GRAVEN IMAGES

GRAVEN IMAGES

Three Original Novellas
of Science Fiction

Edited by
EDWARD L. FERMAN AND
BARRY N. MALZBERG

Thomas Nelson Inc., Publishers
Nashville   New York

Copyright © 1977 by Edward L. Ferman and Barry N. Malzberg

All rights reserved under International and Pan-American Conventions. Published in Nashville, Tennessee, by Thomas Nelson Inc., Publishers, and simultaneously in Don Mills, Ontario, by Thomas Nelson & Sons (Canada) Limited. Manufactured in the United States of America.

First edition

Library of Congress Cataloging in Publication Data

Main entry under title:

Graven images.

CONTENTS: Frede, R. Oh, lovelee appearance of the lass from the north countree.—Grant, C. L. A glow of candles, a unicorn's eye.—Malzberg, B. N. Choral.
  1. Science fiction, American. I. Ferman, Edward L. II. Frede, Richard. Oh, lovelee appearance of the lass from the north countree. 1977. III. Grant, C. L. A glow of candles, a unicorn's eye. 1977. IV. Malzberg, Barry N. Choral. 1977.
PZ1.G78 [PS648.S3] 813'.0876 77-24591
ISBN 0-8407-6557-6

CONTENTS

GRAVEN IMAGES

SCIENCE FICTION AND THE ARTS

The body of science-fiction work about the arts is small but distinguished. Science fiction, as Brian Stableford has pointed out in various essays, has always been a technological fiction, a means of helping us understand the confusing machines and of mapping little way stations, such as showing us where the lavatories might be in the rocket ships—and since its emphasis was on the explication of the machinery, it had very little room for somewhat less urgent matters. Busy, busy: the science-fiction writer felt himself to be a tour guide around the apocalypse. Poetry, music, architecture, sculpture, the dance? Well, these had their value, of course, but they lacked *utility*, to which science fiction was above all dedicated. One can hardly name a single science-fiction story or novel of the forties that had a scene, say, at the concert hall or happened to deal with a poet. ("Thunder and Roses," perhaps, or "In Hiding," where the young genius wrote *Satevepost* stories for easy money.) Mostly, for good or evil, we were part of the machine.

9

But the emphasis changed somewhat around 1950, and continues to shift today. Science fiction has moved away from its roots as a wayward bus through the technology quarter and has begun to grapple with humanistic concerns. If nothing else, stories have appeared about the way in which art will (or will not) survive in the future: "With These Hands" by Cyril Kornbluth, "The Darfstellar" by Walter M. Miller, Jr., "A Work of Art" by James Blish, "The Music Master of Babylon" by Edgar Pangborn.

Painting, music, performance—this anthology is the first, I think, to be exclusively devoted to the subject of art, and so it may constitute a precedent of sorts.

Precedent is what art is about: the breaking of new ground, the granting of the perception to see as we have never seen before, the spiritual insight that will enable us to understand or be moved in different ways. Precedent is not perhaps the business of science fiction, which for the most part seems more than ever dedicated to the smoothing away of strange and terrible landscapes to outposts of Corporate Headquarters . . . and this may be one explanation for the dearth of stories utilizing both art and science fiction.

The three stories in this collection are in various ways a celebration of their writers and themselves, and to the degree that the reader participates in that celebration he knows all of art that any of us can know and, humanized to that extent, may be able to perceive better the limits of his life.

—B.N.M.

OH, LOVELEE APPEARANCE OF THE LASS FROM THE NORTH COUNTREE

BY RICHARD FREDE

Our lead novella concerns an odd couple—a military pilot and a painter—and their search for a vision so majestic that it must be approached in a jet fighter, flying upside down! The story grew from an experience Richard Frede had while researching an upcoming novel called The Pilots. *"I wrote a letter to a friend in the Air Force and one day I found myself at the second and tandem set of controls of an F-106 Delta Dart. At one point in a rather violent maneuver the* EJECT *light seemed to flash on—it may have been an instant of electrical malfunction or it may have been in my imagination. I elected not to eject and, fortunately, my instructor, through my headset, confirmed my decision. But the warning light kept going off in my mind, and I had a lot of recall of the lonely upstate New York countryside over which we did our training. . . ."*

*Richard Frede was born in Albany, New York, in 1934, and grew up in Chattanooga, Tennessee, and in New York City. He graduated from Yale where he was a Scholar of the House in English. He is the author of four novels—*Entry E (*1958*), The Interns (*1960*), The Secret Circus (*1967*), *and* Coming-Out Party (*1969*). He has published stories and poetry and, under two other names, three novels in the mystery-and-suspense genre. He is also a professional photographer and sculptor. His other interests are tennis, skiing, softball, and flying. He lives in Peterborough, New Hampshire, with his wife Barbara and their two sons.*

Flying home alone one afternoon over upper New York State after a couple of hours of practice radar intercepts, Col. Jack ("Jock") McTeague, commanding officer of the 1001st Fighter-Interceptor Squadron, got the urge to slow-roll his F-106 Delta Dart. Having gotten the seventy-foot silver triangle upside down, the colonel was as enveloped within pleasant memories of his childhood as he was encased by his cockpit. So pleasant, in fact, were the sensations of childhood relived that he decided to remain upside down for a little longer.

He found himself looking out at the light and show of a vast low-pressure frontal system moving in like a wall from the southwest. Gray and gloomy and dark and dour at its base, the front was splendid with oranges and reds and streaks of gold and of yellow from a setting sun upon its roof.

He was back in his Tennessee childhood, living on the side of a mountain, his family all Scots and Presbyterians, Highlanders from generations back. When storms came toward the mountain, he liked to climb a favorite tree and hang upside down, like a trapeze artist, knees above him, legs wrapped around a sturdy bough of the tree. He liked to watch the weather from this position: lightning shooting *up* at him instead of down, storm clouds moving in marvelous configurations. Flying along upside down in his F-106, Colonel McTeague could feel again the fearful abrasion of the bark on the tender skin behind his knees, feel the first warm rain on his flushed face, feel the blood pounding in his head.

Ah, the bliss and comfort of the storm and the F-106 and hanging from a tree upside down. The majesty, the *color*. . . . Colonel McTeague righted his aircraft and flew home. It was with an effort that, in the debriefing, he refrained from describing the majesty and color of the approaching storm. But he retained a vision of it and of his silver F-106 Delta Dart hurtling above it, and every so often, of a drinking evening, he would describe the picture to his wife. "I've never been a man for paintings," the colonel would say, "but I'd sure give a lot for a painting of *that*." He said it so often and so enthusiastically that his wife, who had money of her own, decided to give him the painting for Christmas.

"How is that?" said the colonel.

"I'll commission it. It won't be ready for Christmas," his wife said. "But you'll know you're getting it. What I'm going to do is write that art association that advertises they'll get someone to paint a picture of whatever you want in whatever style you want. You know? The American Artists' Association, I think it's called. Mary Culpepper had them do that portrait of her mother. Very successful, too. You know the one?"

"No," said the colonel. "Anyway, this artist probably never saw what I saw."

"You can describe it in a letter."

"He'd have to see it himself," said the colonel.

"Well, you could show him," said his wife.

"I suppose I could."

"Well, I'll write them. I suppose it would be better if I described *sort of* what you saw and what you'd want, so they could pick the right artist for it."

The colonel, who could always decide precisely how to go about getting *anything* done, went to an artists' supply store the next day and looked at color charts.

His wife then wrote to the American Artists' Association, "He says it was generally flaming color, but he could see, as well, sepia, burnt sienna with raw sienna at the edges, and both umbers (burnt and raw), the earth colors, he believes you call them, and oranges . . ."

". . . and some pinks along in there with the oranges, too," Mr. Tribble of the American Artists' Association read. "He believes he saw, too, ranges of rose and vermilion, especially against leadlike gray and blacks. He says especially, too, note the yellow-oranges and burnt-oranges, streaks of yellow, ochers, the yellow-orange family."

"Turner," Mr. Tribble said aloud. Over his desk intercom he said, "Nancy, who is that fellow who does Turner for us?"

"I don't remember," Nancy said. "It's been so long since anyone wanted a Turner. Shall I look him up?"

"Yes, please. And get me his telephone number."

The woman who had written the letter was apparently not without financial resources.

Clarence Beattie awoke to sunlight. His wife, Edna, always forgot to pull the curtains when she got up. One of her many failings. She got up at seven or seven thirty with their little girl and seemed to resent it that Clarence could sleep as late as he wanted, and usually did. So she let the light come in, and he awoke about nine or ten, anyway a good two or three hours before he would have if he'd been allowed to sleep in darker circumstances.

As usual he'd worked the night before, into the early morning, in the next room of their Village brownstone apartment. There was this room where he and Edna slept, the living room where their little girl Grace slept (except when they had company), a kitchen, a bath, and a little room, his studio, where he worked, a somewhat airless room, for he had blocked off the window. He had felt that colors were seeping through it, even at night, and got on the canvas and distorted, for his eyes, the colors he was trying to work with. Summer or winter he was in there in his underwear, a bank of fluorescent lights overhead, painting stylized, hard-edged cityscapes from postcards, which he purchased in shops and at hotel magazine stands that tourists frequented. Occasionally a painting sold. But his usual income was from free-lance commercial work for advertising agencies and magazines—his specialty being topographical illustration. Sometimes, though rarely, he also worked for a commercial artists' group—the American Artists' Association—for which he did surprisingly romantic and poetic and sometimes violent landscapes. He rather enjoyed this work, though it was much out of favor even among the sort of people who patronized the A.A.A., and so the commissions were rare. Once a week he taught perspective at the American Academy. His wife worked part time doing free-lance copyediting for small publishing firms. Their daughter was four years old. They had debts, which never seemed to get reduced—though the creditors changed every so often—of about two thousand dollars.

Every so often, when some unexpected money came in, Clarence would make what he felt to be a conservative investment and then watch the stock go down. There didn't seem to be anything left for him but work and daydreams of sexual adventures with unknown women. Every morning when he awoke now he was once again surprised to find that he was still twenty-six. He felt, physically and in spirit, as if he were getting on toward forty, or even older.

Grace entered the bright room loudly on tiptoes. Seeing him awake she said, "Daddy, you always sleep so late." Clarence turned away. It seemed to him that the accusations of women were the climate and affliction of his entire waking life.

Part of it, of course, was his own fault. Married too early and, to be frank about it, frank with himself, married not only too early, but too modestly. He could have—with a little patience, and knowing what he now thought he knew—he could have done better than Edna. He deserved and should have insisted upon more of a woman, something on the lines of those soft-edged girls who get themselves photographed in the nude by the better men's magazines—or even by the worse magazines. Maybe he shouldn't even be married at all, Clarence thought, and just have girl after girl like the ones in the magazines.

His romantic ambitions, like those of most men who are bored and somewhat nervous, were extreme.

His daughter said to him, "Daddy, why do you always sleep so late?" and Clarence had the strong feeling—not an unusual one recently—that something was going to get him and that there was nothing to protect him from it.

The telephone rang. It was located in the living room and he could hear the ringing clearly enough, but when Edna picked it up and the ringing stopped, he couldn't hear what she said and so had no idea who might be calling. He got down under the covers.

Then Edna came into the room. "It's Mr. Tribble," Edna said. "I think they want you to do a painting."

"The colonel is obviously a madman," Tribble said. "Most of these military people are. That's been my experience. And his wife is *definitely* certifiable. I have a close friend who's a psychiatrist and I'm sure he would agree. *Definitely* certifiable. She accepted the first price I gave her, which, believe me, was exorbitant. By the way, this lunch is on American Artists, so order whatever you want. Another martini?"

"How much did you get?"

"Six thousand."

"My God. Four thousand dollars."

"I was going to ask seventy-five, but I thought that a bit steep."

"I'll have another martini."

"I would have gone to the usual three, of course, if she'd bargained. But she didn't. The commission is satisfactory, of course?"

"Absolutely."

"There's one thing."

"Yes?" said Clarence.

"The colonel insists that you *see,* that you *yourself* see, what he saw. That is, this vision of his he wants you to paint, you're to see it yourself."

"Well, that's usual."

"You'll have to see it upside down in a fighter-interceptor airplane, I gather."

"I don't like to fly." Clarence thought of the four thousand dollars. "All right."

"You'll have to take a special training course, the colonel says. You'll have to see all this from thirty thousand feet or so, and so you have to pass this special training course. He wants to know if you can pass a security clearance, Clarence."

"You can tell him I'm no more secure than any other artist. That's why I'm willing to fly upside down in this airplane of his."

"Clarence, considering the four thousand dollars you are to make out of this, I think a less jocular attitude would be more appropriate."

"How should I know whether I can pass a security clearance?"

"All right. We'll see if you do. Then, if you do, you have to take this training course."

"Yes? Mr. Tribble, do you think I could have another martini sort of to hold on to while you tell me what this course is?"

"Apparently Strategic Air Command gives it, though you'll be flying with Aerospace Defense Command. They're the ones who fly the fighter-interceptor airplanes, you see."

Oh, Lord, Clarence thought. These were names from things like suspense novels and *Time* magazine and the eleven-o'clock news, all of which he avoided.

"Yes. Quite exciting, isn't it? We in the arts seldom get so close to real life, now do we? You're privileged, Clarence, privileged. Imagine what Turner might have done at thirty thousand feet. Yes. Well, you're to go to a SAC base, some airfield as I understand it, and you will be given their high-altitude training course. It has to do with breathing, I understand. And getting out of crippled airplanes in the sky. 'Escape techniques', I believe the colonel called them."

"Oh, Lord," Clarence said out loud.

"Quite interesting, really." Mr. Tribble read from his notes. "High-Altitude Environmental and Physiological Training is what it's called. I don't know of another artist who's ever had it."

Clarence saw himself flying through the sky, leaping into the environment. The feel of it did not suit him physiologically even in the safety of the restaurant.

"The colonel was quite keen on it—the course, that is. You can't fly with him without it. And you can't take the course without obtaining"—Mr. Tribble consulted his notes—"a Federal Aviation Administration Form eight-five-oh-oh dash nine parenthesis one dash sixty-seven close parenthesis," said Mr. Tribble proudly.

"What's that?"

"A third-class medical certificate. It must be obtained from a duly designated flight surgeon. I have located such a person and made an appointment for you."

The doctor's waiting room was steamy and noisy. There didn't seem to be a single pilot in the place. Mostly there were young children with their mothers and silent old ladies by themselves. Everyone seemed to have a cold.

After a while a nurse gave him some vision and hearing tests. Then she returned him to the waiting room, where he waited for another hour, certain he was contracting at least pneumonia amid the sounds of pulmonary disturbances around him.

Finally the doctor gave him a physical examination. When that was concluded and Clarence was dressed again, he sat in front of the doctor's desk and answered a long series of questions that the doctor read from a form.

"Heart trouble, rapid breathing, palpitation?"

"No," said Clarence, his heartbeat and breathing becoming quite rapid.

"Anxiety, depression, nervous disorder?"

"No," said Clarence, beginning to tremble.

"Ever consult a psychiatrist?"

"No," said Clarence, the trembling becoming a shake.

"Well, then, I guess you're fit as a fiddle and ready to fly."

At six in the morning of a cold, black day just after New Year's, Clarence got himself out of a bed in a motel. Six in the morning. He didn't know what rampage his bodily functions might enter upon, gotten into motion so early and so irregularly.

He showered, shaved, and dressed. "Wear an *open*-collar shirt, nothing tight," a sergeant had instructed him over the phone the evening before. Whatever that portended.

The motel coffee shop was not yet open. He found a Dunkin' Donuts along a main highway. The fluorescent lighting, so reminiscent of his own studio, cheered him. Everyone else looked partially asleep or dazed, though he could not tell whether they had just gotten up or were just going home to bed.

At seven he found the appropriate gate to the airfield. The armed guard did not seem concerned about him. Clarence felt that security was not as tight as it might be. Here he was an ardent pacifist and the guard didn't even find him suspect or dangerous. Clarence reflected that if he weren't so thoroughly a pacifist he would rather like to be an officer in the military.

Throughout that day and the next he was addressed by a series of officers and noncoms. They *started*, at seven forty-five that morning, with dry-gas expansion rates, which is pretty heady stuff for an artist at any time.

There followed three days of moisture content in gases, trapped gases, hypoxia, anoxia, Dalton's law, transportation of gases in the bloodstream, respiration and its physiology, emotional effects and affects and qualifications, hyperventilation, Valsalva technique for clearing the eustachian tube in altitude descent, Frenzel technique, Haldane and decompression sickness (Clarence was glad to learn that he would not be allowed to do any flying within twenty-four hours of having done any scuba diving), evolved gas as in bends and central-nervous-system disorders, physiological considerations of age and obesity, alcohol and drugs, injuries and rate of ascent, solid and fluid intake, atmospheres, pressure per square inch of oxygen supply at crew positions, continuous-flow regulators, diluter-demand regulators, ambient air, pressure-demand systems, outboard leaks, subjective symptoms of hypoxia and objective symptoms of hypoxia, emotional symptoms and real symptoms of (it seemed to Clarence) *symptoms,* pressure breathing, hypoxic and stagnant and hypemic and hystoxic hypoxia, emergency settings, left-bayonet connect in two clicks, intercom cord, emergency O_2 *very slow,* stress, skill fatigue, alcohol, dehydration, hyperglycemia, noise, self-medication, circadian rhythms, cardiovascular disease, smoking, rods and cones and optic nerve, spatial disorientation, vestibular apparatus, linear acceleration, prolonged turn, spins, abrupt head movement, rapid acceleration, rapid deceleration, oculogravic illusion, motion/velocity, G forces, transverse G forces, escape.

It was at *escape* that Clarence felt that perhaps four thousand dollars wasn't worth it. They explained to him how to jump out of an airplane. In the air. They explained to him the D-ring of the parachute. They explained to him the orange apple and the quick releases and what to do if the quick releases didn't release. They explained to him the bailout bottle ("—though the Air Force prefers that we now refer to it as the Emergency Oxygen Supply") and how to make sure that it, the O_2 cyclinder, was full. Then the green apple. He had happy thoughts of painting—what with the orange apple and the green apple—but then they were telling him about the distress beacon.

"Remember, the aircraft commander is only going to tell you to jump once. It will probably go like this: 'BAIL *owwwe . . . oot,'* his voice getting quite distant as you see him off and away, and there's not going to be anyone else around to tell you what to do. So when you hear the suggestion that you jump, *jump.* No one else is going to tell you again. Anyone in this class going to be flying in anything but B-52's?"

Clarence raised his hand. Everyone looked at him. He flushed with both pride and embarrassment.

"What you going to be riding in?" the sergeant said.

"F-106," Clarence said, not without noticing that the sergeant's eyes focused more carefully on him.

"Well, they'll give you ejection-seat training before you go up. Just remember, if you have to eject, keep your head back, your arms flat across your chest, and your knees and feet back. Otherwise the panel will shear some of them off."

They went on to the correct way in which to come down by means of the employment of a parachute.

In an altitude chamber, Clarence rode to 43,000 feet and came down to 25,000 feet in fifty-seven seconds. His ears hurt terribly. Under instruction, and still at a pressure altitude of 25,000 feet, he took off his oxygen mask to observe his own symptoms of becoming hypoxic, of losing useful consciousness from lack of oxygen in his bloodstream. His most noticeable reaction, which he was to learn in order to warn himself should his oxygen-system fail, was apprehension. Well, the Air Force called it apprehension. He called it panic. Terror. There he was without pressure putting oxygen into his bloodstream. How the hell could he tell what his normal subjective symptoms of hypoxia might be when he was scared to death? His neighbor turned politely blue, grew a big smile on his face, and passed out.

Then he practiced with minimal oxygen coming out of an emergency bottle. He was instructed that if he breathed it up too fast, he would pass out. But he was so frightened he breathed fast. Waves of warmth passed through his head. Hyperventilation. The mask was so tight and clinging. It collapsed against his nostrils when he drew in breath, making it impossible to take more than a small breath. Claustrophobia wrapped itself around his mind. *He wanted to get out.* And what about those central-nervous-system disorders from lack of oxygen. *He wanted to get out.*

He held on, and just like everyone else, rode safely back down to ground level in the altitude chamber, which had never left the ground anyway.

As if he had not been sufficiently entertained, the Air Force then put him through a rapid decompression. Once again in the chamber, he was blown from a pressure altitude of 8,000 feet to a pressure altitude of 22,000 feet in one half of a second. There was the sound of an explosion and the air turned smoky with ice crystals. After a while he regained his vision and his hearing. They rode back down to the ground.

During all of this he went back to his motel each night, drank a furloughed combat pilot's share of martinis, had some dinner, and dreamed of lack of oxygen and of ejecting. He thought of Edna and of Grace, but they didn't seem very real.

He finished the course with a 92, his mistakes having to do solely with his understanding of escape techniques. These were explained to him again and he drove the four hours home. He couldn't find a parking place for the car and had to put it in a commercial garage and carry his bag five blocks through bitter wind and then up the three flights to their apartment.

When he opened the door he realized that Edna and Grace had had fish for dinner. He himself hadn't eaten yet. And Edna and Grace were out. Thursday night. Edna usually left Grace home with him and went to her Conversational French class. Usually, left alone with him, Grace would neither go to bed nor be quiet. This evening Edna must have taken Grace with her. Or left her with a neighbor. Clarence decided not to inquire.

He was tired, thirsty, and hungry. He was also exultant—at having survived. He didn't feel forty just now. He felt under thirty-five. He went to the refrigerator to get a beer, but before he got there the telephone rang. He went back to the living room.

"Mr. Beattie?"

"Speaking."

"Jock McTeague here, Colonel McTeague."

"Yes, sir."

"How are you?"

"Fine, Colonel. And yourself?"

"Good as usual. So you're all signed off?"

"Pardon?"

"The course. The altitude-chamber course. They told me you finished it up this afternoon."

"Yes, sir. I did."

"Fine. Fine. So you're all ready to take a little spin with me."

"Yes, sir."

"Fine, fine. You've got transportation?"

"A friend lent me a car, if that's what you mean."

"Okay, then, buddy; you just hop in it and come right on up here."

"Right now? It's eight o'clock. And it must be— what?—an eight- or nine-hour drive up there?"

"Yeah, I know. But, Clarence—okay I call you Clarence?"

"Yes, Colonel."

"But, Clarence, I appreciate that it's late and it's a terribly long drive, but there's a *heck* of a front due through here tomorrow, a *heck* of a front, just the thing for you to see. Do you think you can do it?"

"Okay. I'll start out now."

"Good boy! And bring your warm underwear. And did you get your eighty-five-hundred niner?"

"My what?"

"Your class-three medical?"

"Yes, sir," said Clarence, rubbing his card case proudly.

"Whatever gate you get to, ask the guard for the Thousand and First Fighter-Interceptor Squadron, and have him ring over. Someone'll come fetch you."

"Yes, sir."

Clarence wrote a note for Edna and put his overcoat back on. He had one set of long underwear—left over from when he used to ski—and he rolled it up and put it in his bag. That reminded him to take out his dirty laundry and replace it with clean linen and pressed slacks. Then he closed the bag and left. Then he remembered that the military encouraged neatness. He went back into the apartment and shined his shoes. Then he went out again. Once outside the apartment he was conscious that the air didn't smell of fish anymore.

He drove all night. But then, about two hours from his destination, something disconnected from something else that adjusted the intake of . . . Well, he didn't understand any of it; he was just lucky that when the car stopped going, a police car had come upon him and gotten him a tow truck. By the time the car was repaired that afternoon (ninety-six dollars), it was snowing heavily and wildly and the highway was closed. Clarence called the colonel.

"Tough bananas," said the colonel. "Well, you just sit it out, Clarence. Soon's this thing's over and the road's open, you just hustle right up here. There'll be some more weather along soon for us to look at, there always is."

Clarence went to a motel. He called Edna, but no one was home. He went to sleep. When he awoke it was eleven at night. He was ravenous. Before looking for food he dutifully called Edna.

"I'm asleep," Edna said. "Is it important?"

"No."

"Good. Call back tomorrow. Earlier. G'night." And she clicked off.

The restaurant was closed, but the bar was open. It was occupied by a hardy crew of snow-trapped drinkers. Most of them seemed joyous to have had their motoring progress thus arrested. There was a camaraderie such as Clarence had never experienced. Even the bartender was happy. He managed to supply Clarence with two ham-and-cheese sandwiches. Clarence finished them and found himself wide awake. He continued to drink beer and began to take a shy part in the hilarity and celebration going on around him.

An attractive woman, apparently sexually warmed by drink, put her arms around his neck and asked him to dance with her. Clarence was not a dancer, but it was difficult to move anyway. He stood with her and was pleasantly pressed against her by the slight motion and close presence of other would-be dancers. After a while she caressed the back of his neck with her fingertips. She looked at him and said, gently, "Look, if you want to get anywhere, you have to start somewhere."

Clarence said, "Excuse me, but I'm married." In spite of all his dreams of sexual adventure, what, after all, would be the use of staying married to Edna if he was unfaithful to her? "Excuse me," Clarence said and pressed away from her and toward the bar.

The woman looked up at the dark ceiling and said, "Why do men always abandon me?"

Hardly anyone seemed to go to bed. The bartender smiled and laughed and served. Clarence drank beer until he was tired again. He tipped the bartender five dollars. *Five dollars.* The world was becoming unreal.

He arrived at a gate of the Air Force base at three

thirty the next afternoon. He was directed to the Visiting Officers Quarters and, upon signing in, found that he was registered as the guest of Col. J. McTeague of the 1001st Fighter-Interceptor Squadron. A note asked him to call a base extension number after he had settled in.

His room reminded him of his old room in the fraternity house. However, it was considerably better appointed. There was an AM-FM clock radio, a TV set, a desk, a reading chair, and a refrigerator.

A typed notice on the refrigerator read, *This refrigerator is restocked daily with the following. Please check the inventory on arrival so that you will not be charged for usage not your own. Please deposit in the money cup on top of the refrigerator as follows: 35¢ per alcoholic beverage, 15¢ per nonalcoholic beverage. Inventory as follows: 2 bourbon, 2 Scotch, 2 rye, 2 gin, 2 vodka, 2 tomato juice, 2 V-8, 2 quinine, 2 club soda, 2 orange juice, 2 pineapple juice, 4 beer. Thank you.*

Clarence opened the refrigerator. Its interior, nearly empty, was brilliant, light reflecting off shining white surfaces all about. It reminded him comfortably of his studio—in miniature, of course, and colder, but all white and fluorescent and windowless. But there were the little bottles and cans of beverage such as the airlines use. He took out a can of orange juice and popped it open and drank. He closed the refrigerator and put fifteen cents in the money cup. Then he went out in the hall and used the base telephone there.

"Oh, yes, Mr. Beattie, the Colonel's compliments to you. He's presently over at our dispersal area on Cape Cod and then will be flying an exercise to California tomorrow. He expects to be back the day after. Please use any base facilities that aren't restricted. And please charge your meals to the colonel at the Officers' Club.

It's the building next to the VOQ. I'm Lieutenant Stroud and you've got my extension number here and I'm available for any assistance I can give you except when I'm flying."

"Well, why don't we have a drink this afternoon?"

"I'm sorry, I'm flying later."

"I just thought I ought to familiarize myself. I've never been at an Air Force base before. Or any military base."

"Just enjoy yourself and we'll be in touch."

Clarence went back to his room, put fifty cents in the money cup, and made himself a vodka-and-tonic. Then he settled down to read *War And Peace*.

As it happened, the colonel didn't return for three days. Clarence tried to visit the 1001st Fighter-Interceptor Squadron headquarters but was put off. An indifferent Lieutenant Stroud came to have a drink with him at the Officers' Club and had several. "We'd be glad for you to come over and visit with us," said the lieutenant, "but, frankly, we don't know what to do with you. We're not proud, or anything like that, we're just doing our job and, frankly, I can't see you sitting around the mess all day watching us drink coffee. When I say we don't know what to do with you, it's this way. The colonel's got this idea of his. He's going to have you do this painting and he's going to give it to the squadron. Now I think that's real fine. I mean, I went to college and all, so I can appreciate something like that—the painting, I mean. And the sentiment. But man, I bring a *painter* down to our place, what's anybody gonna think? I mean, we're *combat* pilots—what're we goin' to do with a painter? It's all right for the colonel; he's a colonel," said Lieutenant Stroud. "But now *you* tell me, what does a fighter squadron need a painting for?"

So Clarence spent three more days waiting for the colonel and for the colonel's storm. He tried to pace himself carefully, but he found himself drinking before lunch. It tasted so good. And he was so bored. A little Ping-Pong in the game room was about all the excitement he could scare up, here in the midst of adventure. He paced the shots of booze through the five-o'clock radio news and then through the six-o'clock television news. Then he went to the bar in the Officers' Club.

". . . Would you believe I didn't even go there when I was *stationed* there, but my wife insists we go. I mean, I never saw so many tits, and they're all wrestling in the mud . . ." ". . . Well, I thought if I dove for speed and then pulled up with the afterburner and sort of lobbed it at him, the cameras would show I would've gotten him. That was at fifty-two thousand and I couldn't go no higher. But that son of a gun U-2 just kept goin' like I wasn't there, and would've even if I'd been shootin' somethin' real at him. No wonder the U-2's drive the bad guys crazy."

Two drinks there in the bar, but no more because Clarence is *starving*. He hasn't eaten since four or five boring hours earlier. He goes to the dining room and has a huge dinner. Oysters or shrimp to begin with. Wine. Steak or roast beef. He'll show that colonel, sticking him here. The dining room is so sedate. Just families, with children and all, having dinner. "Jimmy, get your mother some salad there." "Sarah, say thank you."

At seven thirty he is finished with dinner, belly distended, time with which nothing to do. He has a brandy in the bar. But there is no one to talk to. He goes back to his room. He reads, "The next day the old prince did not say a word to his daughter." By eight thirty he is asleep. By six in the morning he is awake and bored. He mixes himself a vodka and tomato juice.

At three thirty in the afternoon—just as, in boredom, he was considering going to the refrigerator for his first after-lunch drink (My God, how could anyone drink as much as he was drinking?) he was called to the base telephone in the hallway. He noticed the red Klaxons for the first time. What if they went off?

"Hello?"

"Clarence? Jock McTeague here. Good to hear your voice. How y'makin' out?"

"Fine."

"My boys treatin' you okay? I just got back and I checked with our weather briefers and we got a heck of a front coming through tomorrow. A heck of a front. I should know. I flew through it over Kansas about an hour and a half ago. I tell you, it was splendid. Just the thing for you. All kinds of colors on top of it. Now listen, Clarence, what I'd like you to do is, you hustle over here to the Thousand and First F.I.S. headquarters. You got a base map, don't you?"

"Yes, sir."

"Well, you hustle right over here and get yourself an ejection-seat lecture." The colonel pronounced it "*eeee*-jection." "Just ask for Sergeant Malone, he's expecting you. He's a good man, and he'll straighten you all out and issue your equipment as well. Now I've got a downright burden of paper work awaitin' my immediate attention and I have no idea when I'll be shut of it, but if you don't mind sittin' around after you finish with Sergeant Malone, when I do get finished, you and I could go over to the O.C. and get acquainted. Seein' as how we're goin' to go aviatin' together tomorrow. You willin'?"

"Yes, sir."

"Jolly good," said the colonel, "as a liaison officer used to say to me. Jolly good."

While on base Clarence had discovered the fallacy of a preconceived idea—presumably the remnant of a non-military childhood—that all military people who were not officers were necessarily young. Officers were mature, men below that rank immature. The older you got, the higher the rank you moved to. He was constantly surprised then to find many noncoms significantly older than most of the officers.

When he met Sergeant Malone, Clarence found his being older—he was perhaps forty—quite comforting. The sergeant possessed the knowledge of maturity. The instruction he would give could be relied upon.

He measured Clarence's nose, said "Long narrow," and issued him an oxygen mask. He measured his head and issued him a white helmet with a brown plastic visor, a sunshield. The oxygen mask-communication device was clipped to the helmet, the lines hanging down.

"How's that?" said the sergeant.

"Fine," said Clarence, hearing and feeling his voice inside his head rather than through his ears. It sounded, nevertheless, as if it came from outer space. Clarence himself, in flight suit and boots and gloves, helmet and visor and mask, appeared also to have emanated from outer space. He wished they'd take a picture of him. He wanted to do a hard-edge self-portrait of himself in this guise, though, of course, you couldn't see his face with the visor down.

The sergeant issued him a webbed vest. It was very heavy. It contained survival equipment and was worn over the orange flight suit. They issued him a Russian-style winter fur hat with big flaps that folded up on top.

"You'll need it on the flight line before the colonel lowers the canopy. Afterward slip it into your flight suit. In case you have to eject, you'll need it on the ground. Remember, before you eject, get your head back, chin back, arms in tight across your chest; tuck your hands into your armpits and get your knees and feet tight back against the seat. When you go out, you're going to get *exploded* out and you don't want to lose anything going, like your legs or head. That could ruin your whole day. The parachute has an automatic beeper to tell us where you are on your way down and where you get to on the ground. In the survival kit, which attaches to the ejection seat itself, there's a communications unit like this one." It looked like a miniature walkie-talkie. "Remember to turn off the parachute beeper before you try to communicate. Be sure to raise the antenna. And if you go into trees, remember to keep your hands in your armpits. You get hung up in a tree and can't use your hands, you're in trouble."

"I know," said Clarence, "I had the high-altitude course."

"Good," said the sergeant. "It could save your life, along with what I'm telling you now. You don't know how many people, even the pilots, don't remember to pull in their legs when they're ejecting, and they're a mess afterward, believe me, those who survive. But probably you won't have to."

He fitted Clarence with a parachute. It hung against

and a little below his buttocks and was also very heavy.
It pulled Clarence backward. He had to lean forward
and away from it to maintain balance.

At eight o'clock—his equipment put aside some three
hours before and his body continuing to feel lightened
by its removal—Clarence was still awaiting the colonel.
He sat in the 1001st F.I.S. headquarters and looked at
Air Force magazines. He was glad to see that at least
once a month an Air Force pilot managed skillfully to
bring a crippled aircraft safely back to the ground without further injury to himself or to the aircraft or to anyone
riding with him. There was an award for this accom-
plishment once a month in one of the magazines.

A lieutenant colonel came out of the colonel's office
and suggested that Clarence go on over to the Officers'
Club and have himself a beverage of his choice and some
dinner and await the colonel there—the colonel would
be a while yet. "The paperwork is unbelievable," the
lieutenant colonel said. "You get it done and then half
the time the computer sends it back. That's what we're
working on now. What the computer sent back. The darn
computer can't read plain English." He went back into
Colonel McTeague's office.

After dinner Clarence went down to the bar and drank
brandy. The more brandy he drank, the better he felt
and the less terrified he became of flying and dying the
next day.

Looking into the color of his third or fourth brandy,
Clarence became fascinated by his late—at twenty-six—
entry into the real world, the world where death is not
just a romantic notion cuddled and harbored by a frus-

trated undergraduate, the world where the significant insignificance of being a person is not just an attractive concept of intellectual Europeans who make movies about *not being*.

I have got to remember all this tomorrow, Clarence thought. It's so wise.

He thought of the visored helmet, just like ye knights of olde, and he became very excited. He was going to fly. Ride a horse into the sky like in mythology. Hook up to oxygen and communications systems and wear a parachute, just like the fighter-pilot heroes he had read of when he was a boy. Just like spacemen, just like when chivalry was in flower, just like . . .

"I'm Jock McTeague," said a man in an orange flight suit looming above him. Clarence shook hands with him. "Glad you could make it, Clarence. I appreciate it. What are you drinking?"

"I'll have Scotch now," Clarence said. "Scotch and soda."

"Good," said the colonel, "I'll join you." He nodded to a major who was also wearing a flight suit, and the major went over to the bar to fetch the drinks. "Well, Clarence," the colonel said, "the boys been treating you well? Sorry I couldn't be here sooner." The major returned with the drinks. Clarence now saw that the major was Chinese. "Major Lionel Lee," the colonel said. "Fastest and highest flying Chinese-Hawaiian in the universe."

"As far as we know," said Major Lee.

"No drink, Lionel?"

"My regrets, Colonel. But I'm exhausted. If I had a drink I'd pass out. If the colonel will permit me to say so, you have the stamina of a horse."

"The McTeagues were always first in battle and first to the bar afterward."

"Well, if you'll excuse me, Colonel."

The colonel winked at Clarence. "Of course, after the bar and battle, some of them managed to get to bed, otherwise there wouldn't be any McTeagues today at all, would there? Of course, Lionel. My regards to your lovely lady."

"Thank you, Colonel. Good night. Good night, Mr. . . . er, Clarence."

The major walked off into the gloom not presided over by the light from the silent jukebox.

"I did not always fly entirely in the service of my country," the colonel said. "Before I was married I flew from more than one young lady."

Clarence put his glass down. The blood within him was coursing. He was fearless, joyous in his fearlessness. "I'm really looking forward to tomorrow," Clarence said to the colonel.

"Gallant knight," said the colonel, "the One Thousand and First welcomes ye. Have another drink?"

"Please."

The colonel got the drinks, and when he was reseated, having tasted the elixir to see that it was as ordered, he said, "When I was a little lad, I used to have a daydream. There was this horse. I called it the Evening Horse, because it always came in the evening. It carried me off into the sky. When I was in bed and going to sleep, the Evening Horse would come and carry me off into the sky. To sleep, you see. It was very much like what I saw when I was hanging upside down from the tree in our backyard—"

"Upside down in a tree?" said Clarence, feeling that

his attention might not have been as strict as it might have been.

"Yes. Just as I'll show you tomorrow. You see, I'd ride the Evening Horse going to sleep and see everything I used to see upside down from the tree. You'll enjoy it. It's what I want you to paint.

Clarence wondered, for the first time ever, if he was capable of the task to which he had committed himself.

"I once thought I'd choose that girl to be my wife," said the colonel.

"What girl?" said Clarence, feeling that his mind had strayed upon alcohol and upon the Evening Horse while the colonel had said something else.

"Ah, the lass from the north country," said the colonel, pronouncing it coun*treeee.* "The Evening Horse always carried me to this girl. And then I'd court her. Quite chivalrously, you understand. We were going to be married, I thought. But I was always worried. There always seemed to be something threatening us. But I never knew what. I suspected that it might be that the Evening Horse would go away while I was with her and that he wouldn't come back at all to take me back to my father and mother in the morning. But I knew that couldn't be it. He was an intensely loyal horse." The colonel finished his drink. "Then I grew up and discovered airplanes. Another drink?"

"Gladly," said Clarence. He saw himself at the controls of an airplane, daring the challenges of nature, of combat, of . . .

"Also," said the colonel, sitting down and handing Clarence a drink, "I wanted to touch the fingertips of God. That's one reason a lot of pilots fly. Cheers." The colonel lifted his glass.

Clarence also drank. Either then or some time later, Clarence heard the colonel saying, "I have serious questions about the universe." Clarence looked at his watch. Some time had gone by. He must not have been paying attention. The drink felt cold and refreshing in his throat. His faculties regrouped to listen to the colonel. "I have serious questions about the universe," the colonel was saying. "Also about God. I don't know if He exists. Or ought to. I hope to teach philosophy if I'm passed over."

"Passed over?" said Clarence.

"For promotion," said the colonel, biting an ice cube. "I just want to ask my questions, of someone who can answer them. I don't believe *you* can, *can* you? No, I thought not. We're all just bundles of questions, aren't we?"

Clarence wished himself an understanding of the military mind.

The colonel said, "Tomorrow I will show you wild and bounding skies. There will be a horrible red sunset above it all. Horrid, horrid. Beautiful!" The colonel eyed Clarence dolefully and evenly. "I should never, *never* drink when I'm this tired," the colonel said. He got up.

Clarence followed the colonel out of the bar and out of the building and into the unsettled night, windy and cold, stars disappearing behind scudding clouds.

"Hark, hark, the wind," said the colonel. "Hark, 'tis *God!*"

"I'm going to be a fighter pilot and climb the skies!" cried Clarence.

"Good fellow! If you think this is weather, it's nothing. Wait till I show you the wild and bounding skies of tomorrow."

"And the horrid red sunset!" Clarence insisted.

"And the horrid red sunset!" said the colonel into the wind.

Clarence yelled up at the night, "I'm going to be a fighter pilot and *climb the skies!*"

Hung over, Clarence slept nervously until noon. He ate a careful lunch at the Officers' Club and then went over to the 1001st F.I.S. headquarters. There he sat in the mess and drank mild tea with sugar. After a while he felt better. On one of the walls he noticed a mock shield with a coat of arms. Beneath it was the legend "1001st F.I.S." and above it, "The Flying Knights."

The colonel came in. "Oh, boy," he said, "this is going to be a heck of a show, a *heck* of a show. Gusts up to a hundred, buildups only to thirty thousand. That'll mean the sun'll be on it, like I saw it. Let's suit up."

Clarence climbed up a twenty-foot aluminum ladder, parachute hanging heavily and clumsily behind him. Then, with the colonel's assistance, he got himself into the aft seat of the F-106 cockpit. The colonel made sure the ejection-seat ground safety pin was in place and showed Clarence its position and how to remove it. He showed Clarence the ejection-seat handgrips. "Sit back tight and grasp each with a hand and pull them both up if you have to go," said the colonel. The colonel hooked up Clarence's oxygen and communication leads, clipped together his safety-harness connections, tested his oxygen supply and parachute seatback arrests.

"See ya later," said the colonel.

Clarence watched the colonel climb down from the aft position, walk forward, and then climb up to the forward position. He was a very deft man at going up and coming down and getting into small places. The colonel climbed in and settled himself. He was about eight feet forward, but there was a radar screen directly in front of Clarence and a lot of other equipment in between, so all Clarence could see of the colonel was a bit of white of the back of the colonel's helmet. Clarence was tightly fitted in. It was difficult for him to move. The colonel seemed a great distance away. Clarence, usually most at ease in confinement, such as his studio, now found himself subject to an attack of claustrophobia.

I'm going to be flying at thirty thousand and be claustrophobic there? Clarence asked himself. I am?

Something buzzed and garbled in his helmet. Then again. Then. *"zzzzz . . . zzzzz . . . 's that?"* said the colonel.

"What?" said Clarence.

"*—ll turn it up.* . . . There. How do you read me?"

"Fine."

"Fine," said the colonel. "Just give me a few minutes to get everything checked. There're so many dials and gadgets and things, they confuse me."

Clarence did not laugh.

A few minutes later the colonel said, "Look down and forward of your right-hand console. Tell me if a red light comes on."

"Yes," said Clarence.

"What does it say?" said the colonel.

"It says *Eject.*"

"That's right, that's the bail-out light. If I turn it on, there won't be time for any communication. Just pull your ejection-seat handgrips."

"All right," said Clarence. Though it clearly wasn't.

After a while the engine was started, and the colonel lowered and locked the canopy. The sound of the engine became distant, but Clarence could feel the jet thrust in the aircraft's body.

They taxied out. Before turning onto the end of the runway two men on the ground gave the aircraft a visual inspection. "They call this 'The Last Chance Inspection,' " the colonel said. "I wish they'd call it something else," the colonel said with mock concern. Clarence didn't laugh. "Okay, Clarence, remove the ejection-seat ground safety pin like I showed you." Nervously, expecting to be blown into the air, Clarence removed the ejection-seat safety pin. Nothing happened. "Confirm removal of ejection-seat safety pin," said the colonel.

"I confirm it," said Clarence. "It's out."

The colonel said nothing. They turned off the taxi strip and onto the runway. "Here we go," said the colonel. The engine produced considerable trembling in the aircraft, but they remained in place. Then the colonel released the brakes, and Clarence was mildly jolted against his parachute and seat back.

"Here we go to afterburner," said the colonel. Another jolt. They were traveling swiftly now. The front of the airplane lifted and tilted Clarence so that he was looking toward the sky, but the wheels remained on the ground. Then they were off the ground, moving through air without support. "Gear coming up," the colonel's voice said through the intercom. "Hang on and watch this, Clarence. Max climb. Zero to thirty thousand feet in less than a minute."

The nose came up steeply, and they rushed into the sky. Clarence felt all the pressure against his back. He seemed to be lying on it instead of being seated. In very

little time at all Clarence could see the earth falling away
behind and beneath them. White fields and lakes and
rivers contracted swiftly. The earth lost detail and config-
uration, became a single flat, white field from which
they continued to escape at amazing speed and in wondrous incline. Then it all disappeared and streamers of
gray flicked by. And then the streamers disappeared and
the grayness was complete. Nothing to be seen outside.
No visual indication of motion. No sense of motion except
for the vibration of the aircraft itself. They might not
be moving at all. "We're just through twenty thousand,"
the colonel said.

Some seconds later the grayness lightened and then
became brilliant whiteness. The whiteness was so bright
his eyes teared. Clarence lowered the brown sunvisor of
his helmet.

They broke out into orange and gold and yellow sunlight. Cloud surface gleamed below them. They continued to climb.

"There it is," said the colonel, and he slowly inverted
the aircraft. "Look to your left."

And there, indeed, it was: a bank of cloud, an endless
wave of cloud, rising from gray mists and black darknesses
into a surface crimson and sienna, vermilion and ocher,
just as the colonel had represented. Turner. All his colors
exactly. Just then a light silently blinked on, steady red.
Clarence drew his head and body back, gripped the
ejection-seat handholds, and pulled up.

The canopy exploded away and Clarence was exploded
downward. Looking upward, he saw the tiny, white surface of the colonel's helmet as the colonel remained
in the aircraft.

The helmet was a minuscule white button hurtling

away from him upside down. In his mind Clarence resaw the little red light that had just come on. It did not read EJECT. It read AC GEN.

So much for that, thought Clarence. It was remarkably cold but surprisingly comfortable. In fact, he felt it a pleasant experience falling. Then he remembered that at these altitudes he had a time of useful consciousness of . . . of . . . He couldn't remember. Wouldn't remember. Unless he got oxygen under pressure. He activated the bail-out bottle.

The Air Force prefers to refer to it as Emergency Oxygen Supply, he remembered.

His head cleared—he had not known it was unclear— but the sense of pleasure in falling continued.

The parachute would be automatically activated at 14,000 feet by an aneroid barometer. A while yet. Let's see, it had taken him fifty-seven seconds in the altitude chamber to free fall from 43,000 to 25,000 so . . . The flimsy rubber was sucked tight against his nostrils and mouth, intake of breath impossible. I must breath slowly, Clarence thought. The mask slowly inflated, allowing him to breathe. I must *not* hyperventilate. It still felt pleasant falling. He was in grayness now and was being jostled about. And if the parachute doesn't open automatically at 14,000? he had asked. Well, you activate it manually. How will I know when I'm at 14,000? When trees and houses become distinguishable. Don't open it too early, it'll tear apart when you hit the atmosphere at 14,000. Wait till the atmosphere slows you down. Wait till 14,000 feet.

Clarence looked at what he thought was *down.* Then he looked all about. He was in darkness now. In his mind he had a glimpse of his broker lifting the telephone to

call him to tell him he was suing him for nonpayment
of an order Clarence had called in from the boredom
of the three days on the base.

He was being jostled severely now. All was blackness.
His visor was covered with ice and was frozen shut.
Clarence could not move the turnscrew on top, which
set or loosened the visor. He put his hands under his
armpits and held his boots tightly together and thought
about praying. However, he had never been religious.

There was a *sound?* a *feeling? both?* of explosion, and
his plunge was dramatically arrested. He found himself
holding on to the taut risers of an open parachute. Thank
God, thought Clarence.

He would have to be able to see if he was going to
have any chance for a safe landing. He struggled with
the visor. Incredibly, it cleared, though he was unable
to raise it. Perhaps his body heat, or warmer air closer
to the earth. It was meant to be kept down for the
landing, anyway. That reminded him to free the survival
kit from his body so that he wouldn't break something
in himself by landing on it. It would ride on down with
him anyway, but not against his person.

He was falling in blowing snow. Wonderfully pleasant
feeling, this feeling of falling. Blowing snow. Winds
blowing him, too. What if the parachute crumpled from
an odd angle of wind attack? Now he was swinging back
and forth, back and forth in long, steep arcs beneath
the chute. You have to stop that, Clarence remembered,
before it becomes uncontrollable and you spill all the
air out of the chute. But how do you stop it? He remembered a color movie of a man demonstrating how to stop
that. The man had been falling on a clear blue day.
It looked warm. Ah. Clarence remembered. Pull yourself

up on the risers. One, two, three *up*. One, two, three, *up*. The length and steepness of his swing was reduced.

There was more light. The atmosphere was clearer. The air became sedate and sturdy. The snow continued, but not as severely. Clarence looked down. Wide, flat, white fields under darkness. Scattered clumps of trees. A single house, a single light in it. He judged himself to be at about two thousand feet. He was hanging straight down from the chute canopy now, drifting slowly with the snow toward the farmhouse. There seemed to be no road to it, no roads within sight. They were probably covered with snow. He waited. The air seemed warmer. The descent had become gentle. Clarence was almost thoroughly transfixed by the gentleness of the descent.

Then the ground hurried at him with such speed he thought the parachute had torn open.

He landed on his side in deep snow. Badly bruised, he expected, but he was alive and unbroken. Opening the appropriate clips after some difficulty with his fingers, he detached himself from the parachute. It curled up and blew into some trees.

He had to go to it to turn off the directional beeper so he could get on the communications radio. Which meant he had to retrieve the survival kit he had unhitched from himself.

He went to the trees, all black night and snow above him. There was the farmhouse on the other side of the trees, the single light illuminating a single window. He couldn't find the equipment in the darkness, so he went to the house. He knocked.

A woman opened the door. She wore a long dress of rough material in an old style, as in eighteenth-century paintings of provincial life. Her hair was piled up. She was pretty, but her skin was coarse, from work or weather. Her features had beauty and dignity, but there was a sternness to the set of her expression as if she had just eaten something not to her liking. She said, tonelessly, and as if withholding her belief, "Jack-Jock, my John-John."

"No," said Clarence, "my name is Clarence."

"Jack-Jock," she said quietly. "You've come to me, come back to me."

"May I come in?" said Clarence.

"I thought you'd sunk beneath the wind. You went off in that terrible wind and never came back. No message. But I knew why, did I not, Lord John?"

"I don't know. My name really is Clarence."

"Clarence, Jack, John, Jock. You may come in. Ah, you've come again."

"Thank you. But actually I haven't been here before. Actually I just sort of fell down from the sky."

She said, "It does not surprise me. You were a harper then, did sing of air."

"No, I'm afraid you've got me mistaken for someone else."

"Was it not you who loved catastrophe, Jack-Jock, my John-John?" She smiled at him gently. "Catastrophic beauty, the elements bestirring themselves? Was it not you? Come, sit ye, I'll bring ye wine."

"I'd like that," said Clarence, "I could use that."

There was a fire in a huge fireplace. Clarence took off the heavy survival vest and set it aside with his helmet. The furniture in the room was rude and sparse and large, heavy in leg and arm and back. There was ornate carving on the two chairs. The fabric, too, though worn, had an august quality to it.

She brought drink in a pitcher and handed him a heavy metal goblet. She filled it with a brownish, transparent liquid. Clarence drank. Its strength was considerable. It tasted like liquid made from tobacco and soaked in charcoal. It heated him through, and he thanked her for it. She smiled, refilled the goblet, and drank herself.

" 'They put their spurs into their steeds,' " she said, " 'and each at other fly.' You sang that." She became gay. "You were a harper then, did sing of air."

"Do you have a telephone?" Clarence said, becoming uneasy. "Or a flashlight?"

"And sang ye not, 'Here dwells a knight that never was o'ermatched with any man'?"

"I don't believe so," said Clarence.

"Why, of course you did, John. When you wanted me in the flowers. You were bragging to me. But even so I conserved my flower, did I not, John?"

"I wouldn't know. You've got me confused with someone else. And besides, this conversation is getting unnecessarily sexual."

"You said, 'Let us try our force together.' "

"No, I didn't."

"Oh, you were the warrior, the valiant, harper though you were as well, harper to best attack a damsel's castle, that it were, so concerned were ye, so loving of conquests and victories and jousts and deeds of arms. Oh, deeds of arms, my John-John. What deeds of arms. How you excelled. How you excelled at sport. How you sported and tried yourself. How you sported and tried yourself and excelled at deeds of arms with that fair damsel, my sister. How you put your fingers in her yellow hair and touched her cherry cheeks and kissed her rosy lips and loved her in the flowers and were false lover, demon lover, to both of us."

"Lady, I never did any of that."

"That were overmuch, John. But now the winter's come. I said to myself, 'I will repay in winter.' "

"Hey, lady, really, I didn't do any of that stuff."

"You were cruel, John. My Jack-Jock. Cruel. Away you went in the wind. And I said to myself, 'My love lies in the air.' And I went to my sister. Come, shall we visit with her?"

"Is it far?" said Clarence.

"Below," said the woman. "Beneath and under. Where else? Water is cruel."

Clarence thought about Edna and Grace. He thought about being with them. He found tender indications of love for them within himself. He found exalting affection for them within himself. How comfortable it would be to be with them. How snug and easy, how restful—even if it was Edna's Conversational French night and he was taking care of Grace, and Grace, as usual, was refusing to go to bed or to be quiet. Values and value systems need to be reexamined periodically, Clarence thought, and not just when you're in the presence of a madwoman.

They went beneath the house, down into a substructure where icicles hung from walls of granite block and ice blistered out from the interstices.

The body of a young woman lay on a couch. She was frozen. She was dressed in the same antique fashion as his hostess.

"My sister. But you need no such introduction, having introduced yourself to her in the deepest way. Loved her in the flowers, that fair flower. She has had too much of water. There is no breath within. I held her as you did." The voice was receding, Clarence thought. But he was staring at the frozen body. "I held her beneath me. You held her in summer flowers and I in winter water. All the time I thought, 'My love lies in the air.' "

The voice had receded. He turned. She was standing at the top of the stairs, silhouetted by light from the hallway beyond. "You desire so completely to lie with my sister, now lie with her, John-John. Lie with her tonight, Jack-Jock, for I will see ye sleep with her on the morn, my John-John.

She closed the door and left him in icy darkness with the frozen young woman.

On his hands and knees and by feel, he found his way to and up the stairs. But the door was secure, and without the survival vest he had nothing with which to work upon it. He went down again. He was thirsty from the wine and very cold. He found an icicle and broke it off and sucked on it. He had not expected to sleep, did not want to, but it was so cold, and the enveloping fatigue warmed him and numbed his terror. Remotely and obscurely, his lolling mind remembered that at some time recently he had wanted to sleep in darker circumstances.

He slept.

"Come up, come up, Jack-Jock, my John-John."

She stood at the top of the stairs, a shotgun pointed at him. " 'Tis morning," she said. "Come ye, Lord John. That ye may see where ye shall lie come springtime once again. And every spring thereafter. Hike ye there yourself and spare me the swink of bearing ye there myself. Do it out of love for me, Jack-Jock, me John-John. To the trees, Lord John. To the funeral shroud with which ye came, Lord John."

Clarence stood. He felt rested. His body was not bruised. He was hungry and thirsty. The flight suit was in tatters.

"Come up, come up, Lord John. Make haste, Lord John."

"Look, under the circumstances, I think I'd feel a lot more comfortable if you just called me Clarence. That's really my name."

"Wast not known by any other?"

"No."

"Ever the dissembler, Lord John. Come up now or quit your life now where thou art."

Clarence went up the stairs. In his mind's ear he heard Grace say, "Daddy, why do you always sleep so late?" I won't do it anymore, his mind's voice told Grace. I'll be up early, as early as there is light to see you with. I'll embrace your mother as she sleeps. I'll make breakfast for all of us and I'll be joyful and we'll be happy together. I'll work all morning, and in the afternoon, after lunch and your nap, we'll all go to the park together.

With the shotgun the woman indicated that Clarence was to walk through the hall and out the front door. He decided to run into the room where she had entertained him and retrieve his survival vest and jump out a window and run and see if there was anything in the vest that might help him.

"She said to me, 'Who will care for me until Lord John returns?' and I said to her, 'I will care for you until Lord John returns.' "

The room was empty, his survival vest extracted. He continued down the hall. He felt surprisingly rested, refreshed, and relaxed. He opened the door and went out. The day was gray, cold, heartless.

"I loved her well when she was young. I raised her up. We had no mother then, nor father, either. But Jack-Jock, my John-John, I loved you better than anyone. But ye loved Margret more. Ye took her in the flowers, the sweet, warm flowers . . . and went away. I punished her with water. You see, she couldna swim. But in time she floated back to me."

He was walking in snow, sinking several squeaking inches at every step, across the field to the trees. There was no sign of the parachute. It must be covered over with snow.

He heard a sound of distant throbbing.

Behind him the woman cried out, "Suffer, suffer, cry for deliverance. O waly, waly, my gay goss hawk. This earth shall not be afflicted. Then be extinct, be extinct!"

He heard a huge throbbing from above. He heard wings beating air. He ran. She fired twice, but he was not hit, at least he was still running. She did not fire immediately again, she had to be reloading. The helicopter came down over the trees, presumably homing in on the direction beeper in the buried parachute. Clarence ran toward the trees. Even in the beating noise of the helicopter rotors, he heard the two shots from the shotgun. He was not hit, but the helicopter moved abruptly from where it had hovered to the other side of the trees. Clarence ran through the trees, stumbled through snow.

The helicopter was waiting, a cord lattice dangling down. He grabbed it with both hands and was getting his feet set in it as the helicopter elevated him and delivered him swiftly away.

Some half mile farther on, the helicopter settled him to the ground, cleared itself from where he stood, and then came to the ground itself. The pilot signaled to him and Clarence ran to the helicopter and climbed in. The pilot lifted them off immediately.

The pilot was black, his skin pigment emphasized and framed by the white helmet he wore. He was quick, precise, and casual in flying the helicopter, as casual as Clarence might have been driving along an empty country road.

"Say, that's some beard you got," the pilot called at him. "Must be a foot long. That woman crazy?"

"Insane," Clarence called back.

"She fired a shotgun at me. At the chopper. What you want to go foolin' around with a crazy woman for?"

"I didn't have any choice."

"Yeah. I guess not. I been down myself a couple of times. I didn't know we had anyone down."

"No one reported me?"

"Not to me, they didn't. Fact is, I don't think they knew themselves. I was just coming back from a casual V.I.P. delivery and a controller called me up and said they had a beeper that had just started up on the emergency frequency and could I lock onto it. Heck, I was almost right over it. That woman trying to kill you?"

"To the best of my knowledge."

"Civilians. And in your own country, too."

"You mean Colonel McTeague didn't report me missing? Didn't he get back?"

"McTeague. Colonel McTeague? You mean *General* McTeague?"

"*General* McTeague?"

"He hasn't been on this base since . . . must be seven

years. That's how long it's been since he's made General. He's in Hawaii, last I saw anything about him."

"But the Thousand and First Fighter-Interceptor Squadron—"

"Oh, they're still here. Permanent assignment."

"But McTeague doesn't command it?"

"Colonel Lighthorse Lionel Lee is commander of the Thousand and First."

"Oh, boy," said Clarence.

"You know, something's coming back to me."

"What's that?" said Clarence.

"Oh, only that about seven or eight years ago some civilian ejected himself out of an F-106. Some said he was a fool and some said he was a suicide. But General McTeague, who was flying him at the time, said he was an artist. You wouldn't be that selfsame civilian, would you?"

"Oh, boy," said Clarence.

"Man, I forgot to call them up and tell them I got you."

"Oh, boy," said Clarence.

At the base he was given a complete medical examination. He was debriefed. He was given odds and ends of military clothing. He had become a sergeant, according to his shirt sleeve, a captain according to his tunic. He tried to call his wife, but the number belonged to someone else now, and there was no new listing for himself, for any Mrs. Beattie, or for an Edna or Grace Beattie.

State police were dispatched to the house Clarence and the helicopter pilot described. They were unable to locate it. The helicopter pilot flew a search and was unable to find it himself, even though he knew exactly where it was. Clarence was given a complete psychiatric examination and then was asked to sign a "Hold Harmless" form so that the Air Force could not be held responsbile for anything that had or had not happened to him. He was given a dollar and a carton of cigarettes. It was suggested to the helicopter pilot that he begin considering early retirement.

Colonel Lighthorse Lionel Lee, who vaguely remembered meeting and/or refusing to drink with some artist who might or might not be Clarence, bought Clarence drinks and dinner at the Officers' Club, told Clarence he would give General McTeague a careful written report, and told Clarence he had made arrangements for Clarence to stay overnight at the Visiting Officers' Club. Colonel Lee informed Clarence that Clarence's personal possessions had been returned to his wife "after the accident" and that the car had been returned to Clarence's friend "at some expense to General McTeague. General McTeague will be most interested in all of this," said Colonel Lee. "He always wondered what became of you."

The next morning Clarence was given breakfast at the Officers' Club. He then received military air transport to New York City and the loan of some money for immediate expenses. In New York City, which looked strange to him, because the skyline was significantly changed from that represented on any postcard from which he had ever painted, he learned through a few former friends and professional associates he was able to find and contact that Edna had had him declared legally dead and that she had married again and that she and Grace were living in California.

A GLOW OF CANDLES, A UNICORN'S EYE

BY CHARLES L. GRANT

Mask and shadow are an eternal art, or perhaps they are not. . . . The future may contain enough mask and shadow of its own—it may be a thing that dreams are made of, so as to foreclose the possibility of the performance art. Perhaps. Perhaps not. Upon this and other ambiguities does not only the future but its partial simulacrum, science fiction, repose. C. L. Grant in "A Glow of Candles, A Unicorn's Eye" makes his own statement, which perhaps is sufficient. The future, it is clear, forecloses no possibility from where we dwell.

Charles L. Grant has been publishing science fiction and fantasy for about six years; over thirty short stories have appeared in all of the major magazines and original anthologies, and he is the author of four novels. A former teacher, he is now committed to the somewhat less bucolic life of the full-time writer and lives with his wife and son in Randolph, New Jersey.

There are no gods but those that are muses. You may quote me on that if you are in need of an argument.

It's original. One of the few truly original things I have done with my life, in my life, throughout my life, which has been spent in mostly running. Bad grammar that, I suppose. But nevertheless true for the adverb poorly placed.

And how poorly placed have I been.

Not that I am complaining, you understand. I could have, and with cause, some thirty years ago, and for the first thirty-seven I did—though the causes were much more nebulous. But the complaints I have now are of the softer kind, the kind that grows out of loving, and are meant—in loving—not to be heard, not to be taken seriously.

For example, consider my beard. Helena loved it, once she became accustomed to its prickly assaults. But I do not need it anymore. There is no need for the hiding because I have been forgiven my sins—or so it says here on this elegant paper I must carry with me in case the message has been lost—forgiven my trespasses. But I like the stupid beard now. Its lacing of gray lends a certain dignity to a face that is never the same twice in one week. And it helps me to forget what I am beneath the costumes and the makeup and the words that are not mine. Yet it's not a forgetting that is demanded by remorse, nor is it a forgetting necessitated by a deep and agonizing secret.

It is a forgetting of years, to keep me from weeping.

Because the secret is out.

Has been, in fact, since the first evening I presented this prologue—a device not original, but originally apt.

No secret, then.

But I like the beard anyway.

And so did my Helena, whose hair—such hair!—was once so wonderfully long.

Attend then—or so says the script I no longer need to guide me—but before you decide where applause is warranted, be sure that you understand, be sure that you know exactly what you are applauding. We are still, after all, and in the last sight of the Law, criminals, you know. I nearly murdered, and she nearly surrendered.

And I think that they will catch up with us at the last. Not because we have escaped and were pardoned. But because we have escaped and have been free.

I

Gordon was alone and friendless. . . .

Well, not really, but at the time there wasn't much that I wanted more. I tried to be careful, however, not to disrupt the taping session by allowing my reinforced skepticism and growing discomfort to put lines in my face where character should be, and where, I prayed constantly, it would stay before the bottom dropped out of this market, too, and I had to return to so-called regular employment to build up my account. To cover myself then, I placed right palm to right cheek in what I had been taught was an overt display of not-quite-hopeless despair coupled subtly with the proper degree of Shakespearean melancholy. Then, working at not flinching, I lowered my buttocks onto the conveniently flat rock behind me and stared at the river. They called it a river. Actually, it was something less than two hundred meters of recycled water not nearly deep enough to drown a gnat.

. . . his weary but undaunted brain struggling mightily for the miraculous wherewithal to extricate him from his precarious dilemma. . . .

The subvocal narration buzzing in my left ear so I could follow the cues raised in me first a gagging sensation, then an impulse to swat at a nonexistent fly. I managed to swallow several times without its showing, then shifted my palm to my chin and supported it by resting my elbow on one knee. I could have brought if off. But my concentration slipped. The fact that I was naked, cold, and resignedly anticipating a drenching from the slate-gray clouds massing efficiently overhead goaded me into a mistake. After five minutes of gazing I could not help but frown instead of assuming the attitude of intense problem-solving on the subconscious level. And when it was done, there was no taking it back . . . and I knew it without anyone's prompting.

Unfortunately, no one bothered to turn off the tiger.

I heard it, a grumbling that should have come from the clouds. I rose quickly as it stalked into view, a creature so magnificent in the terror that it instilled that I could not take my eyes from its pelt, its face, the waterlike rippling of its muscles at shoulder and haunch.

A dark-feathered bird swept in front of it, but its gaze did not leave me for even the length of a blink.

Slowly, I backed toward the river, crouched, my fingers hooked into pitiful imitations of claws. Everything inside me from heart to stomach had suddenly become weightless and was floating toward my throat, and I felt a curious giddiness that split the air into fluttering dark spots before coalescing into stripes, massive paws, and disdainful curled lips exposing sharp white death.

It should have leaped when it reached the boulder I had been sitting on. And it did. And despite the training, the quiet talks, the assurances of my continuing good health . . . despite it all, I screamed.

The tiger struck me full on the chest, its front paws grabbing for a hold, its rear claws reaching to disembowel. I fell as I used the creature's momentum to spin us around, dropping off the edge of the low bank and into the water. There were three rows of fire across my ribs, six more on my shoulder blades, but I held the tiger under, a minute, more, until at last it quieted and I thrust it away from me and staggered back to land. The entire sequence could not have lasted more than three minutes from start to finish, but I felt as though a dozen years had been suddenly added to my life. What there was of it.

I fell, gasping, spitting out water, then rolled onto my back and stared at my hands. They were bloody, and I sat up abruptly, looking around wildly for someone to patch me.

This was not supposed to happen.

I was to be strong, clever, luring the beast to its drowning . . . but I was not supposed to be clawed.

Immediately, a white-coated tech raced out from behind me and waded into the water with two assistants, the better to lug the simulacrum back to the shop for another repair job and, I imagined, another shot at another sucker like me. A fourth man, his shirt and trousers rumpled and soiled, wandered over to me and slapped in quick succession antiseptic and medpatches onto my injuries. I smiled at him. He scowled. I knew what was bothering him. If I couldn't be cajoled into doing it again, he would have to do some pretty fancy editing to keep the blood from showing. I think he expected me to feel sorry for him. As though it were my fault.

And when he was done, with not a word of condolence, or even of encouragement, I moved stiffly back to my rock and sat, waiting with dripping hair while those clouds waited to soak me until, finally, the artfully gnarled bole of a beautiful oak on the opposite bank split open with a zipperlike tear, and the director stepped out.

"Great," I muttered, and dropped my hands into my lap.

The director paused for a moment as if reorienting himself, sighed, and retrieved a powered megaphone from the rushes on the riverbank. He sniffed, look everywhere but at me, and yanked a crimson beret down hard over an impossibly battered left ear.

"You're Gordon Anderson, right?" The voice should have been godlike, under the circumstances. Unfortunately, it wasn't. It squeaked.

I nodded.

"You okay?"

Bless you, I thought sourly, and nodded.

"Shouldn't have done that."

I didn't know whether he meant me or the tiger.

"Gordon Anderson," he said again, as if tasting it for some hint of its flavor, or for some trace of its poison.

He stared at the sky, sighed once more, and then I realized I was expected to stand up. That I refused to do. The last time I was naked and standing, my female costar had nearly strangled laughing. It had almost cost me the job, but she had felt sorry for me and blamed it on her lunch.

Besides, those patches weren't new. The antiseptic was weak and I was hurting, badly.

Meanwhile, the squeaking continued.

"Sorry about the animal, but you're supposed to be experienced at this sort of thing, Anderson. That's what they told me at Casting. You're supposed to be experienced. A stage actor, right? You're supposed to know about these things, Anderson, if I know anything about that sort of . . . living. Am I getting through to you, Anderson? You're supposed to know!"

I could think of little more to do at the moment but nod again. My fingers kept returning to the patches, touching, pressing, wondering how I was supposed to handle the flood sequence without ripping open the bandages and bleeding to death. I would see the Diagmed people afterward, of course, but I had a feeling they could do nothing for me. The healing would be speeded up, but there probably would be scars. And why not?

"You're supposed to be brave, yet frightened, Anderson," the voice piped on, as though my screams hadn't been real enough. "Fearless, yet hinting at grave doubts as to your next plan of action. There is a flood coming, Anderson, a *flood!* Do you have any idea what that means?"

"I'll drown," I said, just loud enough for him to misunderstand.

"I don't think you're right for this job, Anderson, to tell you the truth," the director said after a carefully measured dozen beats of pacing, and waiting for word that the tiger was all right. "You . . . you are required, you see, to set an example, the perfect example, for the audience—in case you've forgotten. You must radiate courage, determination, and just a *drop* of apprehension. You have trials yet to come, remember, trials that you cannot possibly imagine. And these trials that you cannot possibly imagine are filling you with challenge and trepidation. And, I might add, those children out there who are watching will want to *be with you!* They have to understand not only the vicissitudes of life, but also their symbolic representations in your journey. If they don't, they're only going to get nightmares. Do you follow me, Anderson? I say, do you follow me?"

Whither thou directeth, midget, I thought, then quickly nodded and raised my hands in a virtuoso combination display of supplication (for the continuance of the job), surrender (to the director's artistic authority), and defiance (for the sole benefit of the tapeman who was still running his idiotic machine).

The director grinned.

I clamped my hands firmly on my knees and straightened to my full sitting height.

"That's fine, Anderson. I knew we would be able to communicate once you got to know me a little better. Now, we have about thirty minutes or so before the flood. Why don't you take a short break and prepare yourself? We can run through the close-ups later on, when the flood goes down. Is that all right with you?"

"Whatever you say, boss," I said. And after he had tramped off somewhere to commune with whatever he communed with to make these tapes, I slid off the rock to the carefully trimmed grass, crossed my legs, and folded my hands over my stomach. After a doubtful glance at the sky, I closed my eyes, wrinkled my brow in practiced concentration, and fell asleep.

When I dreamed, it was of a small glass unicorn surrounded by low-burning candles.

The flood came precisely on cue—the director wouldn't have had it otherwise—but the finely woven strands of safety line that should have prevented me from being swept away into the next sound stage snapped under the pressure. Luckily, I was out of position and managed to grab on to the director's oak, where they found me tightly gripping the trunk when the waters subsided. When I opened my eyes and they realized I was far more frightened than injured, they let me be. Except for the director, who slapped me on the back, patted me slyly on the left cheek (both of them), and strode bellowing off toward the setting of the next scene—the earthquake.

Slowly, testing one limb at a time, I unwrapped myself from the plastic tree and snatched at the robe one of the crewmen held out for me. After a moment's hard glare at the water and the sky, I stumbled off to the dressing room we all used in common. There was no one inside the long, narrow building when I arrived, and for that one small favor I was eternally grateful. I dried myself as best I could with my hands refusing to close, my arms disobeying the commands from my muddled brain; then I sat in front of my mirror and watched a single drop of water fall from my chin.

I stared at my reflection. Stared at the array of small and large jars, long and short tubes, hairpieces and skin dyes, falseflesh and false eyes. Stared at them all until they blurred into a parody of a rainbow; stared, grunted, and swung my fist into their midst, smashing until all were scattered on the floor.

Stared at the mirror, at the reflection, at the high creased forehead and brown eyes and slightly hooked nose and slightly soft chin. My fist came up to my shoulder. Trembled. I wanted to split open my knuckles on that face in the mirror, and drive cracks through the world that existed behind my back.

But at the moment—and only at the moment—it was

all the world I had, and my hand dropped slowly to the table, where it rested on a ragged bit of cloth I used out of habit to wipe off my face.

In the beginning the idea had been a tempting one. Begun by the British and expanded by the Americans, the tapes were the foundation of a dream-induced system through which young people would hopefully be matured without actually suffering through the birth pangs of adolescence. Hospital wards with soft colors, nurses with kind faces, and for two hours and twenty minutes every other day the young were wired and hooked and taped to a machine, which I and others like me, those actors with no place to go, inhabited. We wrestled with tigers, endured floods, endured women and men and disasters personal. It was, as the narration stressed again and again and again—who knows how often?—all very symbolic, and all very real.

Watch! the voice ordered.

Take care, the voice cautioned.

Watch, and take care, and listen, and apply . . . apply . . . apply . . . listen . . . apply . . .

A debriefing, then, which lasted for something like an hour. More, if you were new to growing without aging. Less, if you'd been in the system for a year or more.

The first children/adults would not be through the entire program for, the director once told me, at least another ten months. But, if you listened to him carefully and believed his raving, things were moving along just splendidly.

I could see it without much prompting.

Eleven-year-olds with graying hair and wrinkles and a walk that bordered on the burlesque of infirmity.

A girl twelve with the mind of a woman.

A boy ten with the rebellion sponged—exorcised out of him, exorcised and leaving him without dreams of how it had been when he had been . . . but he never had been . . . young.

It was, admittedly, exciting. And the nightmares I had about the possible consequences were only just that. So I rationalized whenever I went to the studio. After all, frankly, it was a job. An actor's job. Just about the only one left.

I had been in Lofrisco, wandering about that coast-long cityplex, when Vivian-my-agent called me and brought me back to Philayork. It was *the break,* she told me confidently—the chance for exposure, and the cash, that I needed.

"Listen, Gordy," she'd said, "these kids will know you for the rest of their lives! Not by name, but they'll recognize your face! They'll want to see you on stage—if that's what you're still after—on the comunit channels, the cinema bowls. You'll have it made, you idiot. You can't pass this up."

And, to be honest, I hadn't. But neither had I forgotten the near-empty houses I had played to when I had managed to wheedle permission to leave those joyhall holovid arenas and cinema bowls.

Near empty.

Partially full.

There had been five in which I was an understudy. I didn't much care. It was live, actors and audience, and I drifted from one theater to another waiting for the chance to get in on the action. But they all folded in less than a month, the audiences deserting them long before the last curtain. Drifting in, stalking out, curious more than anything, and no one bothered to wait for the players who slunk from their failures from unlocked stage doors. Several times I tried to ask someone just why he was leaving, but never got an answer that cured the question.

Finally, when I cornered one of the directors and demanded to know why her play was a failure, she only snapped an arm toward the gap that was the stage and shrugged. "I guess we're running out of gimmicks. We need a new one. I don't know. The way things are going, I don't really care."

The Storm's Eye had three dozen sets, and auditorium seats that slowly tilted back to focus audience attention on a holovid simulation of the typhoon threatening the actors on stage.

Great World Yearning had catapults and springboards, trapezes, and a 360-degree stage.

Blessing had four orchestras, three tenors, waterfalls, ceiling storms, a marching band, rehearsals for the audience's instrument parts, and a prominent reviewer who insisted on getting every name in the theater for his comprehensive critique.

Take This Crown had seventy-nine speaking parts and four burnings at the stake.

Where Hath God Raged had a planetarium, an esper-narrator, and a colonist from the Moon.

Three playwright/producers had created them all. And when the last one gave up hope, I took the slip marking the deposit to my account and wandered from theater to theater. Something, I knew, had died in both artist and observer. Then, taking the easy way out, I managed to locate and assault with tears and fists all three of the creators one by one. All in darkness, I sought out those so-called playwrights, and after each attack I fled until my lungs burned me to a halt.

My justification at the time was simple: They were murderers, of something I could not yet understand. They had been part of a conspiracy to kill off words.

I wandered, waiting to be caught for my crime, listening for the accusing scream of a WatchDog swooping angrily beneath the Walkways, netting me, lifting me, locking me away.

I had to have been mad to have done it. But there were no still and small voices directing my attacks, no sudden blind fury that drove me to the call of insanity that guided my hand, only those questions, all beginning with *why?* and the knowledge that the playwrights had been midwives to disaster, had birthed disasters before, and were part and parcel of what I knew was the dying of a dying art.

Yet there was no feeling of catharsis.

I had done it.

Nothing more.

So I sat in front of the dressing-room mirror and thought of the tiger and its claws, and of the tiny director who was forcing me unknowing to remember.

It was a play within a play within a play within a dream.

Like a beautiful thing I had seen once, and from which all I could remember was a tiny, shattered, fragile glass unicorn.

I pushed away from the table and dressed as best I could with the patches pulling at my shoulders and ribs. My fingers fumbled as I snapped my shirt closed. My thighs were elastic as I slipped on my boots. Sooner or

later I would have to tell someone what I had done.
There had been nothing on the news and, though I
wondered, I kept silent.

But not for long.

Helena.

A studio flyer took me to the entrance of my Keyloft
and, once inside the lobby, I sagged against the liftube
frame and held on. Looking down. Looking up. Rising
free, falling free. No need to worry, Gordon, old son,
the magics of science will give you faith.

2

I had been born, raised, and eventually cast willingly
adrift in Philayork, the largest of the East Coast city-
plexes. My father was the owner/manager of a joyhall
which, in addition to the usual game rooms, gaming
rooms, and stunt rooms, had a small cinema arena. None
of the major features played there, but the minor ones
were nevertheless sufficient to lure me from spools and
tapes, to spend days and hours drifting through the stories
that holoed around me. It wasn't the technics that en-
snared me, enraptured me, but the men and women who
portrayed the characters, and the men and women who
paid their small admissions to eavesdrop on the plots.

("Marta, over here, hurry! Listen to what this guy is
saying about the Count." "You listen, Will, I'm trying
to find out what happened to the Colonel. We'll meet
by the Grand Canyon when I'm done.")

They all knew it was sham and that they could if

they wished put their hands through heads and cannon fire and the rings of Saturn or the domes on the Moon. But naturally they wouldn't. They listened, compared notes, reconstructed stories, and returned for what they had missed.

By the time I was in University, I succumbed to a temptation, which was easy enough since I knew most of the plots by rote. I stole time here, sleep there, and several times managed to last through nearly three quarters of a show before anyone realized I wasn't part of the action. The idea that I could be something and someone I wasn't intrigued me. I did research, spent time in regular theaters in the less-visited parts of the city, and changed my emphasis in University without telling my father. When he did find out, and heard my dreams, one of us lost, and I left.

Studied. Learned.

Discovered agents and sold myself to Vivian. Who laughed at my studies. (*"My God, Gordy, nobody needs a script on the stage anymore; who told you you needed to learn how to memorize?"*) She took me quite literally in hand and showed me what show business was, outside of the school.

For eighteen years, then, I managed a fairly steady and obviously unspectacular living playing that man over there in the corner talking to the beautiful blonde, and that wounded trooper crawling through the Martian sandstorm, and that body, and that face, and . . . and. Until, between takes, I found myself wandering back into theaters that had stages and audiences and waterfalls and . . . and . . .

There's nothing to say that would stand alone as a

reason. I loved it, that's all. Loved it, and hated it, because it didn't take long for me to see that something was wrong. Lethally wrong.

"You're crazy, you know that, Gordon."

"Just get me the jobs, Viv, that's all I ask."

"It takes a special kind of training. I've told you it's not like learning lines from a holovid script!"

"I'll learn."

"But, Gordon, you'll have to improvise! That's all the whole thing is, except for the effects. You're given an outline and you bluff your way through it. It takes years to learn it right."

"I've done it before, you know that. What's the big fuss? You'll get your percentage."

"You don't get it, do you?"

"I'll learn. That's all there is to it."

"You don't get it at all."

There was a wave of nostalgia that had, for the briefest of lightning-lit moments, the old-style theaters rejuvenated, rejoicing, rehiring actors and producers and directors and such. Lord, how we tried. But the wave flattened, and by the time I was making those dream-tapes for children, nothing was left but the must, the dust, and the drifting in and out.

3

I went into my home: living room, bedroom, alcoves for lav and ovenwall. All in shades of black and white.

I ate, not tasting, and stared at the Keylofts across the street. I watched a news summary and discovered the playwrights I had attacked were recovering. Euphemisms abounded, but the message was the same: person or persons unknown.

God, I wished that hadn't been so bloody damned true.

And fifteen minutes later, Philip and Helena came for a visit and I fed them their eager rations of stories about my taping day. All the time watching Helena, as though Philip were only a ghost along for the ride.

"He sounds like an insect I worked for once," Philip said of the director. Philip was fifteen years older than my own thirty-seven (Helena was four years younger). He enjoyed reminiscing about the, as he called it, flesh-and-blood theater he had been in, but it was a dream that he lived—Helena told me he had been a minor bit player who seldom had lines and was lucky to find two weeks' work in fifty. I don't know why, perhaps because of Helena, but he liked me. "An insect, Gordon. Stamp him out. You won't miss him. I promise you."

"Oh, don't be a fool," Helena muttered. "He has to finish the contract." She was sitting cross-legged in the center of the floor, swirling a snifter half full of a brandy I had hoped to save for another, more special, occasion. Not that just being able to look at her wasn't special—and the moment I thought that was the first time I realized that I'd fallen in love. "Gordy, you can't pass up that money, you know. I mean, that's as far as it goes. No money, no food. How much simpler can it get?"

Philip, who was portly and conscientiously pompous, nodded and retrenched, scratching at his hairless scalp. "She's right, you know. There's no sense ranting about artistic integrity when you have to provide bread for the table."

"It isn't fair," I mumbled.

"Nobody said it was, man. But then, nothing ever is. There is no such creature as a Universal Fair, and I'm absolutely stunned that you haven't learned that by now. I mean, son, there you are, aren't you? Beating your head against the wall, trying to live on, of all things, the stage theater. You can scream all you want to about its lamented demise, but there's nothing you can do about it. Nothing at all."

I could only tug at my chin and gaze at the ceiling. It was true—God!—that the year of the Romantic had closed eons ago. No more traveling shows to the towns between the plexes, and only a single course in stage history at University, while the instructors told me sadly that the art was falling apart. But it wasn't. It was falling in, like a building whose inner supports had been dissolved in acid. A flurry of subsidies provided a revival or two, but essentially only prolonged the collapse, and when the charities took over most of the funding, there was a death knell unmistakable along the length of the aisles.

I closed my eyes and rubbed them, wishing Philip would banish himself so I could talk to Helena.

I smiled then when she crawled over to sit beside me, a gentle white hand resting on my calf, massaging absently.

"Gordy, if you drop out now—"

"Helena, I don't think Gordon wants to hear any more."

I sat up quickly. There was something in the big man's voice, a warning. I frowned and looked to Helena, who was brushing a finger idly through the carpet's low nap.

"Gordy, let's face it," she said without looking up,

"if you cut from the contract, Vivian will let you go. And if she does, you'll end up like us. Like me. And like Philip."

"And what," he demanded loudly, "is wrong with the way we are managing? We hang in, don't we? We've been—"

"Starving, you idiot," she snapped. "And I won't have Gordy going the same way."

"Starving?" Philip's laugh was singularly mirthless. He punched lightly at his stomach and stretched out his hands to exhibit the fat that clung to them. "One doesn't starve, girl, and still look like that."

"You know what I mean. Starving for work."

"We manage, I told you."

"We manage, we manage," she mimicked in a high, child's voice. She looked back to me, and the gray in her eyes had slowly shifted to black. "One part between us, Gordy, since June. One stinking part, and the thing folded before the first week was over. He refuses to . . . what's the word? condescend? . . . refuses to condescend to do the work you do. He's a fine one to talk about artistic integrity. And he's fat because he takes most of the food dole in starches. He has a Falstaff complex, Vivian says."

"I refuse to listen to this—"

"Then don't," she yelled. "Go back to your loft and improvise something. Improvise thin. And don't call me, Philip. My vione is closed, for the duration."

"Helena, I will not be spoken to in—"

I'd had enough, more than enough. I unwound from the couch and moved to Philip's side. It helped that I was a full head taller and that my weight was distributed to give me at least the illusion of strength in my chest and arms. But the illusion was all I needed, and Philip fumbled into a meek silence.

"I can't help it," he finally said, almost whining. "Vivian fired us today."

I blinked dumbly, turned around to Helena, who was still on the floor. If I had been struck with a steel pipe I couldn't have been more stunned.

But: "True," she said. "She says she can't live on a percentage of nothing."

"But I am still man enough," Philip persisted as he looked for a way to regain the advantage, "I am still man enough not to have to condone the manner in which you two have—"

I shut him up by grabbing his arm and nearly dragging him to the door. He was too surprised to say anything. I slid the door back, eased him out, and stood there to be sure he entered the liftube.

"You'll pay for this, Gordon," he warned as he descended. "I am not without influence in some . . ."

I laughed and held on to the door frame. "That line is older than all of us put together, Philip. Why don't you just get yourself a job. In a restaurant." I had to shout the last, since he had already dropped from view, but the noise made me feel better. Somewhat, anyway. And I closed the door quietly, instead of slamming it.

Get a job.

Helena came up behind me then, reached to my shoulders and massaged them skillfully while she rested her cheek against my back. I closed my eyes for a moment, then took a calming deep breath and began talking. Explaining. Describing. Telling her everything and knowing that if she wanted to, she could run out to the

Blues and probably collect a reward. The police were always giving out rewards. It was part of the system of mutual cooperation and protection. I stopped my confession only once, when her hands left my shoulder. But I finished. And when I was done, everything that had been keeping me upright deserted me. I sagged. She caught me and led me into the bedroom. And this time there was a catharsis of a sort. The weight of the attempted murders was, not lifted, but lessened. And I'm ashamed to admit that I was doubly relieved that she had not run to the Blues, for the reward.

And when we lay on the bed, each to a side, and did not touch or attempt to peel off our clothes, I knew she did not pity me, but loved me instead.

"I can't believe they're not really dead," I said into the darkness when the silence grew too long for me to accept. "But from the report I heard—and would you believe it was only just before you came here?—from what I heard, none of them will be the same when they recover. The worst part is: now that I've told you I don't feel guilty anymore. And that's got to be wrong! I wonder if I should stick around until I'm caught. I'm bound to be, you know. One of them must have seen something. And if my name and picture go out through the network, there's no place I can hide. Not for long, anyway."

"But Gordy, it's been nearly two weeks. If the police knew something, they'd be busting already."

I smiled. Grinned. Shook my head even though I knew she couldn't see it. "What's their hurry? I haven't tried to leave the country."

"Maybe . . . maybe you were lucky. Maybe they didn't know who it was, didn't recognize you, I mean."

I rolled over onto my side, one arm up against my

cheek. I tried to see her, but couldn't. But I saw her anyway. "I keep telling myself that. It's a hope, I guess. I wish I knew."

"Gordy?"

"I'm awake."

"Are you wondering if I hate you for what you did? I mean, I did a show for one of them a year or so ago."

"A little, I think."

"Well, it's dumb, but I don't. I'm a bit frightened, though."

"I know that one well enough, don't I? Two weeks, and I still can't figure out why I did it."

"You were angry. Furious. That's obvious enough."

"Sure, but why? It wasn't the first time I was ever in a flop." I worked at a laugh, then, to take the sting out. "When you think about it, I guess, they're all flops, aren't they?"

"Of course they are. You just don't know why."

"Gordy, I want to help you."

"Escape?"

"No. I want to find out what's going wrong. I don't want it to happen. I . . . I have some scripts in my loft. I keep them under the bed, and when I get too depressed I read them."

"Scripts I don't need, believe me."

"No, not those kind. I mean real play scripts. Shakespeare, Williams, Miller, Chekhov . . . people like that. I'll bet I have more than two dozen of them. I got them . . . well, let's say they just gravitated into my gorgeous little fingers when I was visiting friends . . . places."

"God, Helena, you're a crook!"

"Look who's talking. It's funny, Gordy, but I'll bet
I know almost every line of them by heart. It must have
been nice, not to have to make up things as you went
along. It's all down there, just like your cinema things.
'When beggars die there are no comets seen.' You sure
can't improvise something like that, can you?"

"Who said that?"

"I don't know. Miller, maybe. I don't remember."

"You should."

"Why? Who cares besides you and me?"

"What about the guy who wrote it?"

I drifted back and forth from a sleep filled with candles
and unicorns, and when I asked Helena about it, she
told me the scene was from something about a hundred
and seventy years old. She quoted me a long passage
from the end of the play, about worlds lit by lightning
and change and things like that. I'm no history buff,
so I can't say how appropriate that might have been
to the time it appeared, but I know about lightning
now. And when I tried to explain it to her, all I could
do was choke and tell her never mind.

Finally, just before dawn took the black from the ocean
outside the plex, I cupped and pillowed my hands behind
my head and whistled softly a song I once knew. It would
have been nice if it had been a lullaby my father used
to sing. Would have been. But it wasn't.

"Helena, there's one thing I know, now."

"What? And don't you ever get tired?"

"No, not often. And what I know is: we're dying. You
and me and Philip and the rest of the whole stupid stable.
Now that's a good word: stable. We're horses, Helena,

in a motorcar world. One by one they're shooting us down. These tapes I'm making, they're supposed to be helping kids grow up. And what do I do? Me, the hero who survives floods and earthquakes and invasions of god-awful monsters? Just like a kid I lash out and hit someone just because I don't get it. I almost killed those guys, Helena. And they'll come for me. Someday."

A rustling. The bedclothes. Helena had finally given up and slipped in between the sheets. "Then we'll have to escape. It's as simple as that."

"We?"

"Oh, come on, Gordy! Do you think I'm going to let you have all the fun?"

This time the laughter was real, delightfully so, and I stretched out, gathered her to me, and we rocked, like children, until the spasms had passed and we were sober again.

"Look," I said, "there's no sense in my making some big dramatic escape until, and unless, the Blues come for me. It'll be easy to hide in a plex this big, right? And I want to finish the contract so I can get a job somewhere else if I have to. I don't need that blot on my work record, not now. And I have to find something else out. Like you said, sort of: I want to rate a comet. Even a small one. And to do it, I'll have to learn every-thing I can about why we're . . . dying."

"I know the answer already."

"Sure."

"The public doesn't like us anymore. It took a few thousand years, but they've finally decided they don't want us to live."

"No," I said, hovering close to an answer, yet not close enough to know what I was seeing. "No, there's something more. And before I start running, I want to know what."

"Then the first thing you're going to have to do is not to be so solemn. If we're going to hunt for this thing of yours, we'd better do it smiling."

"Why?"

"Oh, go to sleep, Gordon. You're no fun anymore."

Two days later a pamph came, announcing the limited engagement of a series of original material to be performed by players from one of the lunar domes. I had seen them before. I needed to see them again, knowing without knowing that they held the key. Vivian got me the tickets, and I repaid her by showing that simp of a director just how good an actor I could be. He loved me. I loved me. And, thankfully, I still wasn't picked up by a WatchDog patrol. I still jumped at shadows, still looked over my shoulder, but I was beginning to believe that I would always remain free. Or so I tried telling myself each night before sleeping.

The second day after the Lunar pamph came, I was stopped in the Keyloft lobby by my landlord, who told me there was a friend of mine waiting upstairs.

"He didn't have a latch, Mr. Anderson," he said, "but I seen him around here a lot of times so I figured you wouldn't mind that I tubed up and let him in."

I nodded thoughtfully, thanked him for his kindness, and spent most of the time in the liftube wondering if maybe it had been a Blue plant, and my dear old landlord would be collecting that reward.

But it wasn't.

It was Philip.

He was just signing off the vione when I came in,

and as fast as I stepped around the couch to see who he was talking to, he shifted his bulk until the screen staticked into darkness.

"What?" I said, perching on the couch's arm.

Philip spread his arms in an attitude of peace-making. I didn't believe it for a minute. Without a single direct word, I had taken Helena from him, and had made him admit twice that he was living a deadly romantic lie. The friendship we had had was buried. Deep.

"Come on, Phil, I'm hungry, and then I have some studying to do for tomorrow." Half true. After eating, I was going to continue reading some of the scripts Helena had let me borrow.

"All right, then," he said, still standing by the vione. "I've come to inform you that I overheard something this morning that I believe you would be interested in. In return, I expect a favor."

"I don't get it," I said. "You want to make some kind of deal?"

He nodded.

"For what? A lousy favor? What do you need, money? A place to stay?"

"Just wait a moment, Gordon, and you'll find out everything. I am, as you well know, currently unemployed. According to procedure, just being part of Vivian's client menagerie marked me employed. When she unceremoniously, and without real cause, dumped me, I had to gain a measure of strength and make myself known to the nearest Blue Station Local to . . . to sign up for the complete dole." His hands fluttered, clasping at his stomach, grabbing at the baggy trousers he hadn't bothered to tuck into his boots. He was all in green today, his lucky color.

"I'm sorry, Phil."

His grin was short-lived and insincere. "I'm sure you are. But that's not the point, is it? While I was there I overheard a couple of the Locals—one was a 'Dog pilot, I think—talking about a series of criminal attacks down in the old district. Where you hang out, Gordon. I imagine you've heard about them."

I nodded, slowly, my face a masterpiece of serenity.

"Well, one of them was a regular patron of . . ." He rolled his eyes in an effort to display to me how distasteful his words were. To him. Not for me. "He enjoyed spending many off-duty hours in a joyhall." The words came in a rush, as if acidic on his tongue. "Arena stuff. You know what I mean. The sagas and things that you are always blathering about."

"Phil," I said, rising and heading for the ovenwall, "if you're going to be snide, just show yourself out, okay? I don't need that kind of aggravation today."

"I'm sorry," he said, standing behind me as I selected my lastmeal, and pointedly made the selection for one. When I turned around, he shrugged. "The Local was saying that he was sure that one of the actors fit the description of the man—they think those things were done by one man, you see—of the man who did them. Of course, I couldn't hear what the man looked like."

He stopped. I waited.

"I thought you might like to know."

"Oh? What for?"

"Well, really, Gordon, you holo folk stick together like I don't know what. I thought you might like to put out the word to your friends, have them watch their backs. So to speak."

I kept my hands in my pockets—clenched, to keep

them from trembling. I nodded, hoping to appear contrite and grateful simultaneously, and led him toward the door.

"The favor?"

"What favor?" I said. "Oh. Well, sure. What is it?"

He took my arm at the elbow, his fat hand tight, the fingers pinching. "Please, talk to Vivian, won't you? I can't stand having to beg for a meal every day. I mean—really, Gordon, it's so demeaning, if you know what I mean."

"Philip, Vivian could get you a dozen parts tomorrow if you would only let her. But you won't. And until you do, there's nothing I can do, either."

He stepped back as if I had slapped him. Then, a scowl as dark as midnight crowding his face, he shouldered by me into the corridor outside the loft. He took a step toward the liftube, looked back over his shoulder, and smiled.

"You'd force me to do that, wouldn't you?"

"Phil, I'm not forcing you to do a thing. You want me to ask Vivian to let you back, you'll have to compromise. That, my friend, is all there is to it."

"I'm sorry for you then," he said, and left.

I waited for him to make a reappearance—waited, then hurried back into the loft and made a careful search to see if he had taken anything, disturbed anything. The only evidence he'd been there, however, was the pamph. It had been picked up from my couch, obviously read, and tossed onto the floor. I retrieved it, folded it into quarters, and stuffed it into my pocket. It had on it the date Vivian had gotten me the tickets, and the man I was to see to pick them up.

I felt sorry for Philip and his nonsense ways, but had

more important things to worry about at the time. I ate rapidly, watched the news for indications of impending arrests, then called Helena and we spent the rest of the night tying up the vione, reading random scenes from the scripts she had lent me. I would read a line and try to stump her for the next. I seldom won, but what was more important: I was learning them myself, and moving about the room grandly, until she snapped once that I kept disappearing from the vione's range.

It was, without a doubt or a worry, the single best way to pass the time—short of actually having her in my arms, of course.

That, I promised her a dozen times during the night, would come later. And often.

And all the time, that hovering I had felt drew more steady, closer, and the answering light more clear.

At last, a week later, I stood in front of the theater in the park. It was a low dome, black and silver and sprouting several cowllike entrances through which people were already filing. A mosaic apron in blue, gold, and white led up to the dome, and from its center rose a tall post with four huge spotlights. Their soft glare was somewhat reassuring, but it turned the surrounding foliage into a dense black wall.

"Gordon!"

My name was like a slap across the back of my head. I stiffened, not knowing whether to run or surrender, then turned. It was Helena who stepped out of the shadows. Lithe, she looked uncommonly lovely in a plain gray tunic and trousers. Her auburn hair was almost like a veil. I held out my hands and she grasped them, pulled me close, and we kissed, once, lightly, forever.

Then I told her about Philip's visit, and she shattered her loveliness with a vicious scowl. "Relax," I said, rubbing at her arm. "The most he can do is swear a lot."

The floodlights dimmed twice.

"Time, great hunter," she said. "No more stalling."

There were dozens of gold guidelights hovering at the head of each aisle. I held up my tickets and one of them brightened and led us to our seats, seats in an auditorium that radiated back from a traditional stage. I mentally blessed poor Vivian's efforts, crossed my legs, and held Helena's hand. Waiting. Staring at the proscenium, which was studded with holovid representations of the solar system, each planet revolving in truncated orbit, the moon in its center, dotted with blue specks that marked the colonist's domes. I was impressed, and depressed. I was cold, unusually so, and I could not figure out just why this was so.

I tried concentrating on the curtains, on the flecks of crimson that flashed whenever a guidelight flittted too close.

I tried listening to the audience around me, its muffled laughter, gossip, scoldings, coughing.

Something.

Something.

I knew it was there, but when I tried to drive it away so I could enjoy the show, it balked as if yanking on my arm to tell me something far more important.

Music, then, and I was distracted.

And three quarters of the way through the first act, it all fell into place, solidly, painfully, so that with some mumbled excuse to Helena, I crept up the aisle and hurried outside.

Walked. Paced, rather, in a large circle around the lightpost. There was no doubt that the performance was something I would never forget—if novelties are things from which memories are spun. The company was expert, the same I had seen those long months ago, and this particular oarkdome had been reconstructed to approximate and give semblance to the absense of gravity the players were accustomed to on their own home satellite.

It was, in one dark sense, beautiful.

On the stage they were in all manner of costume. Free. Floating. Swimming. A free-form exercise complete with sets and speeches. The women were pale snowflakes drifting around men who were the same. I hadn't been able to follow the story very well—something about a starship lost around Andromeda—but many times there were long pauses in the action and in the flow of words, and the children in the audience grew restless and whispered. As did the adults by the time I had left. I could see, then, that before it was done, few would be listening to the dialogue magnified and booming. They would be watching only—and for that they all could have just as easily attended a joyhall show.

The play was a circus.

The Lunars were freaks.

That was why the people came. And that, I finally understood, was why they want to other plays, in theaters, on stages. I was a freak. A freak who happened to be around when volcanoes erupted or a ceilingstorm thundered or the sets changed so rapidly it gave one a headache. There was no longer any discipline, either in players or audience, no feel for words, because the words were instantaneous.

It was stupid. I should have seen it before. It was

obvious, so obvious that I had overlooked it in search of something far more complicated, far less damning.

What did the man say? The man who broke the unicorn of my dreams and who tries now to blow out my candles? A world something by lightning. Well, I was struck.

And I was . . . I was mad.

The nightwind chilled suddenly. An arthritic attendant with a small pouch at his side shambled around the area looking for debris to justify his pension. But the apron was clean and he vanished without once looking up at me, disappearing around the theater dome curve. A clock figure, I thought, with no hours to chime.

I scowled then, and shook myself like a drenched dog. I was falling too quickly into a self-pitying morbid mood that would do me no good if I wanted to devise some way to reverse the trend I had so belatedly discovered. I decided to get Helena and take us home, and had already started for the entrance when I stopped, a peculiar whining bothering my ears. I rubbed lightly at my temples, and the whining grew louder. Familiar. Another step, and I glanced up and saw the spiderleg spotlights walking a WatchDog toward the place where I was standing.

Frozen for a moment, I stood like an idiot until I realized they'd be landing not far from where I stood. I bolted into the theater and pressed myself against the door frame, watching as the sleek black-and-gold police machine settled onto the heart of the mosaic like a bloated dragonfly. A Blue leaped out, steadied himself, and reached up a hand to assist the others following.

There were only eight that I could see, standing around in a curious display of alert watchfulness and indecisiveness. Then my nails dug unfelt into my legs. Philip lumbered from the exit, disdainfully brushing away an offer of assistance. I must have lost my temper, and a good part of my reason, because I found myself standing just outside then, and when a pinlight suddenly flared and caught me, Philip pointed.

A bell, small and unobtrusive, sounded behind me. Intermission had begun.

The Blues had already taken their stuntons from their waists, and I could see by the glowing tips that they were going to kill me if they had to.

Ah, you fat-bellied Judas, I thought, and spun back inside, fighting my way through the people seeking exit, grabbing at Helena's wrist when I saw her. I dragged her several meters before she tried to pull back, but all I had to do was yell "Blues" into her ear and she was with me, running down the aisle toward the curtains. Without bothering to stop and think, I vaulted onto the stage, hauled her after me, and raced into the wings and along the narrow corridor I knew would run the length of the theater's rear wall. There was a great deal of commotion back in the auditorium, and though I wanted just a moment to think things out, to ask Helena for advice, I slammed up against the fire exit and went through without stopping. A handful of Blues darted around the corner, yelling when they spotted us, but before they could set their stuntons for a firing charge, we were through the trees and into the underbrush so thoughtfully managed to make our flight easier.

Suddenly I stopped and Helena yelped. Except for

the faint glow of the theater's lights, the darkness here was complete and, falsely or not, I felt a momentary safety.

"What?" she whispered as we heard the 'Dog's whining pitch as it lifted from the clearing.

The darkness was complete, I thought, and if we continued headlong as we were, we would be bound for injury that would make a mockery of our trying. I slapped impatiently at my thigh, then took her hand and made my way back, angling in a crouch toward the front of the dome.

The WatchDog whine screamed.

Handheld spotlights shattered through leaves and branches.

With only eight Blues immediately available, I knew my chances of at least getting to the park gates were fairly good. But it had to be done quickly, before reinforcements were summoned. I whispered all this to Helena as we moved, the words snapping singly, like those of a sprinter out of breath. Twice we had to duck out of the way of the thinly spread cordon, but soon enough we were at the clearing. The playgoers had already been herded back inside, and only Philip remained, talking quietly with an officer who was holding a comunit circuit in his hand. Instinctively, I took a step toward them, but Helena jerked me back.

"Later," she hissed in my ear. "And save a piece for me."

It was pleasantly obvious from the dour expression on the officer's face that we weren't going to be easily caught—if at all. Emboldened, then, I made my way through the trees to the pathway I had taken only a brief hour earlier. A minute's waiting that seemed twice a lifetime, and we broke from the cover and into a steady trot. We ran on our toes to keep the echoes from betraying us, and left the path only when we came to a bend too acute to enable us clear sight ahead, or to skirt the now unfortunately well-lighted gardens.

I thought of Philip, wondering how, until I remembered the mailer with dates and names scribbled on it.

I thought of him again, and wondered why, until I remembered his pride and the beating I had given it. Well, at least he would have the reward, I thought with a grin, though how much good it would do him was moot, since I had every intention of getting away.

I grinned even wider. Intentions. I had intended so many, perhaps too many things in these first thirty-seven years. And this was the first time I had actually been driven to action, to do something, to move. I almost felt good, I almost felt joyous.

And the feeling lasted until, only twenty or so meters from the gate, we had to veer sharply into the brush. A Blue had suddenly come from streetside and planted himself directly in front of the only way we had now of leaving the park. Dropping to the ground, I ground knuckles into my cheekbone, trying to force through the pain something I could use to eliminate that man before he was doubled, tripled, made unassailable.

We crept closer. The shouts behind us had separated, nearly vanished. Once, the WatchDog sailed above us, above us and beyond, back into the park. Then Helena jabbed me on the arm with a finger and pointed at the Blue. At herself. She made a steadying motion with her palm and rose to her feet before I could stop her. I tried a lunge, but it was too late. She was already in the middle of the path and walking toward the gates, her legs affect-

ing a slightly drunken gait, one hand brushing through
her hair, the other angled out from her side as if providing
balance.

As she moved, then, so did I. Staying within the
boundary of the hedging along the path, I made it to
within five meters of the Blue before I had to stop—and
watch—my hands pressed to the ground, ignoring the
sharp digging of pebbles cutting into my skin.

Listening to the 'Dog still circling above.

Helena began an off-key whistling, and the Blue almost
dropped into an offensive crouch, then saw her and
straightened. She giggled, hiccuped—I thought she was
overdoing it more than a little—and reached with one
finger to unseam her tunic. The Blue raised a warning
hand, cautioning her to remain where she was. She giggled again, lurched forward, and swayed. The Blue—a
young man who should have known better, but didn't
because he was young—took that first important step
toward her. She swayed again, then allowed her knees
to buckle. The Blue moved instinctively, catching her
around the waist, allowing her weight to carry him
around and down, his knees not quite touching the
ground.

Immediately he moved, however, so did I again, this
time racing from the brush to get behind him, and before
he had completed his dipping motion, I had his stunton
in hand. Fumbling with the studs on the handgrip of
the cylinder, I tried to set the electric charge as low as
I could. Then I lay the tip alongside the Blue's head.
He jerked as Helena wriggled out of his grasp. He jerked,
his arms snapping back, his hands almost touching at
the base of his spine. Jerked, his tongue protruding and
his breath inhaling in one explosive wheeze.

A silent dance while I was too dumbfounded to run. Ending.

"Come on," I said more harshly than I had intended, and with Helena's assistance I dragged him into the bushes.

"Into the breach, isn't that what they say?" she asked me as we clasped hands once more and raced for the nearest Walkway.

"Who says?"

"Who cares?"

"You're not making sense."

It was apparent that neither of our lofts would be safe for us any longer. I had no doubt that Philip had also told the police about Helena's involvement with me. They'd be looking for her, too, once they'd discovered she wasn't coming home. But the Walkway had its terminus at the edge of the cityplex, and from there it was only normal highways for landcars and hovercats. They were only sparsely used, of course, for the villages and towns not linked into a plex, but walking them was unthinkable, especially at night.

So it was less a coincidence than has been reported that we ended up at Vivian's place less than an hour later.

"I'm leaving," I told her after we'd barged in and cornered her on a chair near her bedroom. "Sorry about the dream-tapes and all, but we're in rather a hurry."

She was too surprised to do more than blink, then quickly gathered her dignity about her like the gold-and-green robe she wore to cover her weight. "I heard on that"—she nodded toward the comunit—"that you were wanted. God, Gordy, what made you do a thing like that?"

"I don't know. I wanted to be a star."

"There aren't any anymore, but you're too thick to know it."

"I know one thing, Viv," I said, "and that's *why.*"

"So? Tell me."

"Viv," I said when Helena coughed, "one last favor. The keys to your landcar."

"What will you do if I don't? Beat me to death?"

I shook my head, rose, and after a moment's long agony, she reached into a drawer in the table beside her and tossed me the keys as though they were hot. "I'll report the thing stolen, you know."

I laughed, moved as though to kiss her, then joined Helena, who was already in the hall.

"Listen," Viv shouted suddenly from the doorway, "if you get a job, remember you're still my client!"

The vehicle was an old one, but it got us through the plex tunnels to the outside, and once on the highway with no 'Dogs in our wake, I managed to slow down a bit. But we ran, through valleys of trees that had no hand to arrange them, past dimly lighted villages where we dared not stop. Twice in four hours we passed other vehicles, all going in the opposite direction, and each time I felt as if I would strangle until the headlights glared by and we were in darkness again.

Helena sat quietly in the passenger seat keeping watch on the starred sky. She was pale, far more pale than I had ever seen her now that the excitement had given way to realization. I kept telling myself that she had done nothing wrong, that she could easily go back to Philayork and claim I had taken her by force, or some such nonsense. I kept telling myself that as though it were a prayer.

And finally her weariness caught up with me and I had to find a small clearing at the side of the road. When I did, I pulled over and, without so much as a kiss or a wink, I fell asleep.

This time, there were no dreams.

4

We rode for two days more, staying away from the main arteries, sticking to the tinier, less-traveled roads that webbed off the highway. It was difficult at first for several reasons. The hardest adjustment was to the continuing sky, the mountains, the sudden inducement of vertigo when the road would suddenly bend and drop and we were faced with a broad and green valley several kilometers wide. And now that we were running, we abruptly realized that we had no place to go. No friends. No contacts. Only the certain belief that should we attempt to enter a cityplex again, we would be trapped as fast as we walked into the first restaurant for something to eat.

Only Helena and I, then, and some half-formed hopes.

And finally, a small town called Eisentor, where we grabbed what courage we could and stopped. With what money we had we bought provisions, some clothes, and extra fuel for the car. No one asked us questions, no one paid us any more mind than they would a taxman drifting through his rounds. When it became obvious that we weren't suddenly going to be jumped and shackled, we relaxed, found a small eatshop, and had us a decent meal. We said little, however, because the fear of the flight was still ghosting around our eyes. We ate, only, and drank what we could.

Then we walked awhile through narrow streets with wooden, brick, or clayboard houses. We sat on a bench and watched several children playing around a puddle left over from the previous night's rain.

Suddenly, without consulting Helena, I walked over to the children and asked them what their favorite shows on the comunit were. They didn't seem too eager to talk to a stranger, but they answered me anyway; and when I did a few lines from one of the plays Helena had given me, did a few lines and some comic strutting, they laughed. They were puzzled, to be sure, because they didn't really know why, but they laughed and asked for more.

I gave it to them, as much as I could, but when I saw their mother peering anxiously from behind a nearby house, I excused myself and hurried to get Helena.

"Did you see that?" I said excitedly as we made our way back to the car. "Did you see those kids?"

Helena kept nodding as I kept repeating the questions, and when she finally lay a hand across my chest to shut me up, I still couldn't stop grinning.

"Feels good, does it?" she asked smugly, as though she already knew the answer but was making me say it.

"Well, of course it does," I said. "But . . ."

"But what?"

"I don't know. It feels good, and it feels . . . funny." I scratched at my head, my throat, moved rapidly away from the edge of the sidewalk when a hovercat aired by, its skirts keeping down the blow of brown dust from its fans. "Things ought to be banned," I muttered as I brushed at my trousers.

"Progress," she said. "But what do you mean, 'funny'? You've acted before. What's . . . I don't know what's funny about it?"

When we reached the vehicle still parked in front of the eatshop, I hadn't yet found an answer. I thought about it, thought about what I had learned from the Lunar production, and from Philip and Vivian, trying right there in the middle of that town to squeeze in, in one way or another, the last piece.

To put together, as Helena said much later, years later, the last fragile piece of a broken unicorn.

And when I did I hustled her into her seat, slid quickly behind the wheel, and drove off much faster than I thought I was going. A few heads turned, a few faces frowned as we sped through Eisentor and back into the hills, and as soon as I realized it I eased the acceleration. The one thing I didn't need now was to have our faces remembered.

"All right," I said as I turned onto another side road, "I have to find a place where I can do some thinking."

"Isn't there anything else you do but think?"

Her bitterness amazed me, so much so that I almost stopped right there.

"I mean, Gordy, aren't you getting tired? Didn't those people . . . didn't they do anything for you?"

I made excuses for her. She was overtired—we'd hardly gotten the best of rest, sleeping in the car or on the ground beside it. She was still overwrought from our flight. She had not yet been able to accept the status she had willingly, knowingly, adopted when she came with me.

I made excuses, but for the next two hours or so we

argued. About little things, dumb things, sniping and picking until it was apparent one of us was going to leap from the car if we didn't calm down.

By nightfall, I knew she was ready to give up. Maybe she had thought I had a meticulous plan already worked out; maybe she thought there was still some vestige of romance in weariness and hunger, dirt and thirst. Whatever it was, it angered me, and I was just about ready to turn around from wherever we were and take her back to Philayork when I realized that if I did, if I gave her up without some sort of trying, I would be no better than Philip and his incredible paunch.

I slowed and began to talk, ignoring her gibes as best I could, noticing after a while that they grew fewer and less acid. I talked, roughing out the idea I had had when prompted by the children. Her skepticism fed on it for nearly an hour, but I refused to give it up. And when I was done, with all her objections buried in the darkness around us, she was silent.

Shortly afterward, we came upon a solitary abandoned house, one of many that belonged to those who, having no direct contact with any of the smaller towns, decided that perhaps the plexes weren't so bad after all. Those we had come across before had been done in by the weather or vandals or a brutal combination of both, but this one had recently been vacated, and it didn't take me long to force my way in. There were scant provisions left in the ovenwall, but they were enough to fill us. The comunit still worked and, while I made some effort to hide the car, Helena watched the news for some sign of our escapade, and much later, years later, we both admitted that our egos were blunted sorely when nothing was broadcast. We were minor criminals then, it seemed, not worth the airtime.

We slept in the tiny bedroom. Apart. Alone.

I began to have doubts.

"We'll have to stay here for a few days," I said the next morning. "Just to be sure. I want to be completely sure before we go on."

"It happened too fast, Gordy," she said. We were sitting opposite each other in the living room. Her eyes were swollen and red, her hair in uncaring disarray. "Everything was moving just nicely, slowly. I guess that's what I mean. Then you showed up, and all of a sudden I couldn't blink without something happening. You know, we didn't even have time to say—"

"We had no one to say it to, really, you know."

"There was Vivian, I suppose. I guess we said good-bye to her. In a way."

"But she fired you!"

"She was still someone I knew."

"Well, for all that, so am I."

"Yes, but you're here."

"You really think we can get away with it, don't you?"

"Why not? We won't have some thirty-room loft overlooking the ocean, but we'll manage. It all depends on your priorities."

"We'll have to change, then, won't we?"

"I'm afraid so. Not radically, mind you, but enough to confuse anyone we might happen to meet that knew us."

"Now what are the odds of that, Mr. Anderson?"

"Fantastically small."

"Do you have any idea how many years it took for this hair to get this long? You're asking an awful lot of me."

"That, too, depends on your priorities."

"If you're not careful, Gordon Anderson, you're going to get as pompous as Philip. Hand me that knife."

"The food's running out. They must have disconnected the supply when they moved. Must have? Of course they did. I must be getting stircrazy or something. It's all that practicing you're making me do."

"Well, if the food's running out, then we might as well start planning to make our first move. You know, Philip said he was starving. I wish he'd walk through that door right now. I'd tie him permanently to a chair and face him to the ovenwall. Then I'd smash the thing and let him watch the food rot while he shriveled."

"You're vicious."

"I have a sense of the dramatic."

"Do you like the color of my hair? Black sets off my skin rather nicely, don't you think?"

"Do you like my beard? Vivian kept telling me I had an agreeably weak chin."

"Helena!"

"What's the matter, don't you like it?"

"Where . . . where did you get it?"

"There's a storage room upstairs. I was looking for some clothes, those over there, and I found this little chest. I think there must have been children here sometime. A long time ago. Anyway, I opened it, and there were all these baubles and things. This one was at the bottom."

"I can't . . . it would look better on you."

"No. It's yours. See? It has a chain around its neck, just like a halter. You can wear it around yours. For luck."

"It's too small, Helena. I'll break it."

"I'm not going to argue with you. You'll wear it and like it. If someone asks you, you can tell them you have a fetish for horses."

"They'll know it's not a horse."

"I wouldn't bet on it. Besides, you and I are the only ones it'll matter to, anyway."

"It matters to you?"

"If it doesn't, I've learned all those parts for nothing, haven't I? You know something, Gordy, you really can be dense sometimes. You really can. Now put it on."

"I feel funny."

"Don't. Just wear it."

"It's so small, it's buried in my palm."

"Wear it! It'll keep the beasts away."

It did.

5

I stood at the rear wall of the meetinghouse. I think, that year, it was somewhere in Michigan. In front of me were several rows of static chairs dragged in by volunteers from the attics and storerooms that had been opened to us when we arrived. Already there was a fair crowd waiting. Talking. Nudging with elbows. Pointing with

only half-hearted disdain at the crudely painted backdrop on the far wall. It depicted, rather impres-
sionistically, a forest none of them believed existed, but
a forest nevertheless. They drifted in and smiled when
handing me their admission, but promptly forgot I was
there once the money had changed hands. Which was
perfectly all right with me. I had worked toward that
end. Now I could watch them without fear of being
rude—gauging, searching their faces, estimating their
average age and income, style, and education.

Most of the time my conclusions were correct, and
the material that would be presented to the audience,
numbering just under fifty, would be geared to whatever
imagination I thought they possessed. It was a skill, and
a necessary one, that I had developed over the years after
we nearly landed in the clutches of the local Blues the
first time we tried our little show. We had hoped that
anything in those scripts Helena had stolen would be
sufficient to enthrall. Sadly, and realistically, it didn't
work out that way. Luckily, however, we'd been given
a second chance, and after I had had an opportunity
to talk with those who had come to see us that night,
I knew which of our plays they would enjoy the most.

We did it.

And they did.

It was simple, actually, once I understood that even
in the towns the audiences had been . . . not spoiled,
but despoiled.

We worked out a routine then, which grew into a
science. A week or so in each community. The first night
an informal education. The second a performance with
intermittent explanation. The third through the fifth or
sixth something done in earnest.

No gimmicks.

Just words.

And that crudely painted backdrop became a forest indeed.

We grew. A boy here, a young woman there, an elderly couple with young stars in their eyes. But it was, as always at the last, Helena and I—and our children when they grew.

Philip came to see us one evening, trailing behind a representative of some official or other who, having heard of our little troupe, had come to see. I had been nervous throughout the entire performance, thinking that fat and now enfeebled old man had pursued his idiot revenge to the extreme. But when we were done, Helena and I were given some papers in which, with much legal phrasing and hyperbole almost sickening, we were granted our pardons. Artistic merit had rehabilitated us, I gathered. The only catch: we were not allowed back in a cityplex, for any reason, at any time. And I think Philip was truly enraged when both Helena and I accepted the terms. Laughing.

I sighed silently. I waited until I was sure there would be no late-comers, then lifted a finger, which dimmed the lights. Working swiftly and carefully then, I adjusted the makeshift spots that had been bolted for us over the lintel of the meetingroom door. And once lighted, the forest became natural, and once populated, it lost what was artificial in the words of the players.

There were no curtains, so we walked our exits.

There were no musicians, so we improvised our songs.

And the costumes we used were bits of rags, shards of cloaks, and sometimes only the clothes on our backs.

I watched from the back, waiting for my cue, and

as I did, I took from beneath my shirt the gift Helena had given me when we had given birth to our dream. It sat in my palm, glowing, its eyes catching the light like two miniature candles.

And when my cue came from Helena, the laughter was real.

"When beggars die, there are no comets seen," Helena has said. It was her favorite line.

Helena.

Is dead.

Last year.

She was eighty.

But my favorite line . . . "I didn't go to the moon—I went much further—for time is the longest distance between two points."

She was eighty.

Prologues and epilogues.

I give them alone.

But no matter how often my world is lit by that lightning—I'll not now, nor will I ever, blow out my candles. When all is done, and done . . . and done, a tiny glass unicorn still sits on my palm.

CHORAL

BY BARRY N. MALZBERG

Writing introductions is always risky work. The story, if it is of any value, should include the introduction, so what, ultimately, is the need of one at all? But writing introductions to one's own fiction must be doubly or triply risky. What, after all, is there to say? Just the biographical details, I suppose. The story—which in certain ways plays with and perhaps extends themes that I have admired in the work of the talented Alfred Bester—is conscientious in structure and fairly energetic in style, and that is already more than enough.

*Biographical details: I was born July 24, 1939, and have been a resident in a New Jersey suburb near the Ridgefield Park Oil Dump & Refinery for several years. Married, two children. Have been a professional writer since 1966, with twenty-five novels and a hundred and fifty short stories sold in science fiction, one of which (*Beyond Apollo, *1972) won the John Campbell Memorial Award, a mixed blessing, but a blessing just the same. Currently, I am phasing down my career in science fiction but* *am willing enough to keep a hand in. One of my main interests is music, not only because I like music (is this not like saying one "likes air"?) but because I am a recent reenlistee in the beaten but energetic ranks of second violinists in third-rank orchestras. I played the violin here and there from 1954 to 1963, but gave it up for a dozen years for no reason that seems even vaguely defensible. In 1975 I returned to it and have since gotten back to my own (negligible) performance level. Nothing in all my agonizing career ever gave me a tenth of the pleasure that one rehearsal ever did, and that is a truth which evades not only my critics but has also managed to evade me for many years as well, to my regret.*

I admire Beethoven, and when I was fifteen years old I thought that might be a nice kind of life to live: tragic, heroic, immortal, beloved, neglected and scorned but brilliant—all of that kind of thing. Until very much later I failed to see that being Beethoven would have, over all, involved pain, a pain that would supersede during the lifetime the work itself. I no longer wish to be Beethoven, but I did enjoy playing the Fifth Symphony last February with the orchestra, and I wouldn't miss the Violin Concerto for anything. His Ninth is to me (the one unchanging factor in my life since sixteen) the greatest piece of music ever written.

Scherzo

Allegro ma non troppo un poco maestoso

The Heiligenstadt Testament, though—that was a killer. Complain, complain, Reuter thought. Renunciation of this and dismissal of that; ruminations about death, the weather, Napoleon, and over all the matter of the deafness, which was beginning to be something of a bore. Since it never really came to anything, since

it never interfered with the work (that was for sure),
why make such a point of it?

But history, unfortunately, was inflexible. Every Traveler knew that. Once you began to jiggle with details,
even the smallest, let alone the really big stuff like deafness, you risked losing hold of large pieces of history and
then the world itself washed away. We live on a pen-
insula, surrounded by the waters, held to land only by
the one thin tendril of a continuous past, Reuter thought.
And pain. Now that was pretty good. It was certainly
a lot more interesting than this babble: he'd like to
include that.

But, no. He was here to do what he was here to do:
therefore, the Heiligenstadt. Hunched over the papers
on the third floor of his stinking, reeking rooms in the
Vienna of 1802, Reuter applied himself to the paper.
I renounce, he wrote, *I renounce.* How did that go in
German? It didn't matter, the papers would be picked
up and the translation done by his section man, but he
would feel a little more secure if he knew German. A
hint of authenticity. For that matter, he would feel a
little more secure if he knew more music, but then again
you had to keep some sense of perspective. What he knew
about was history and the psychology of the mind that
would have been Beethoven's. The rest could be faked,
right down to the transcripts of the compositions, which
he had stowed in various cubicles in the room. Nothing
had to be original; all he had to do was to reconstitute.
He supposed.

Renuncia? No, that was Spanish. *Renonissement?* Probably
no such word existed, although his execrable French
would have been preferable to nonexistent German. *I
renounce all of it,* he wrote, *I can no longer go on. The truth
of the matter is that I am rapidly going deaf, and with the*

*loss of that sense comes the loss of the sense of my art. I am
a fraud, a mockery. I am no longer Beethoven.*

He flung the pencil from him, put his hands on the
paper, lurched upright from the desk. The trouble was
that he could no longer take this stuff seriously. Napoleon,
JFK, Thomas Alva Guinzaburg—there were personalities
that you could really get yourself into. Even some of
the minor composers like Ravel or Chamberwit had at
least some balance, some range of personality. But Beethoven—and you might as well face it—had only two
moods: self-pity and heroism, and both of them at the
cheapest and most superficial level. Twenty-five years
more of this would drive him insane and toward death,
just as they had driven the original. Even with the accel-
erative device he wondered if he could last out the two
months necessary for the key points.

Enough, Reuter thought, enough. I can pick it up later.
And he took his filthy frock coat and went out into the
streets of Vienna. Perhaps a little piece of sausage. Perhaps he would look up his nephew, Karl. Oh, no. No
Karl for another fifteen years or so—that was right.

Molto vivace

At his final briefing the Directors had been explicit
to Reuter, even threatening. "We have noticed, both in
the interviews and in some of the continuing testing
procedures, that you are showing a certain querulous-
ness—perhaps the word is even resistance—toward the
occupation of Traveler," one of them had said. All of
them had said. One or the other or the next of them
had said. One of his problems was that he had always
had difficulty in individuating the Board; they seemed
very much like one another.

In the most technological culture of human history, Reuter realized that he had a suspicion and fear of technology. It fitted him for his occupation, but still . . .

"Reevaluation is constant," they had said. "You are free to withdraw at any time, even now. If it makes you unhappy, you should not have to do it. Also it interferes severely with your function. The Traveler is not a robot, you know; you are not merely making checkpoints. What you do, you have to do with conviction. If the feeling is gone, we cannot trust the work."

"No," Reuter had said, "It's all right. I want to continue. You know that I do this well."

"We also know that one cannot be a Traveler indefinitely, and there comes a time when, if that is not seen, we have to make our own judgments."

"I understand that. No," Reuter had said, "it's just Beethoven. Being Beethoven, I mean. I must admit that I have little sympathy for the subject. I don't actively dislike him, but I can't get inside the persona."

"Then withdraw," the Board said. "Dislike means a failure of conviction, and if somewhere in Vienna you are *not* Beethoven even for a moment—"

"No," Reuter had said, "I've done all the research, I've been primed. It would just go to waste if I withdrew now. I can find the role with conviction; it's just that it makes me unhappy. But then again that's purely a problem in the performance. I'll work it out."

"You'll have to," the Board had said, "and you'll have to avoid repetitions of this in the future." For people of their importance in the Department of Reconstruction, the Board had always struck Reuter as being curiously tentative; even now he could always win arguments with them. But then again he had come to realize that the Department of Reconstruction was regarded by many in the Institutes as an eccentric, minor, perhaps even neurotic outpost for cranks. In addition, the Board had little self-respect, which made it difficult for them to keep their positions absolute. "You're under constant review," the Board had finished. "This is a continual process, just as the matter of Reconstruction is itself. Life is a process. No positions can be absolute; no Traveler lasts forever."

"I understand," Reuter had said. "I will take it under advisement. I will be a proper Beethoven. I will be a good Beethoven in full conviction," he had finished. And he had turned from them and gone out of the sterile enclosure of the great and impressive room in which the Board sat (the Institutes had done as well for the minor Departments as for the major) and into the great teeming wildness of the Buenos Aires of the twenty-third century. This century—and he had to believe it—he was trying to hold together, piece by piece, as were all of the Travelers, by living the history that gave the Institutes, that gave the terrible, and mystifying world into which he had been born.

Adagio molto e cantabile

"A piece of liverwurst," he said in English to the old woman behind the counter, "and some plain hard rolls. Perhaps a little sausage as well if it is tender. I love tender sausage." He hoped that the translator was working; the woman looked at him in brief incomprehension before he realized that she was more than a little deaf herself.

"Piece of liverwurst," he shouted, pointing, "and some tender sausage." Never mind the rolls.

The woman said "Ah!" and, leaning under the filthy

counter, took out a reeking piece of meat. *Pfui.* He would have to get rid of this garbage before he even took it back to the room; no one could survive with that smell in his nose. At least the Board would not object, not strongly, to that. The policies were inflexible: one walked the corridors of the past and acted in them with conviction, but one partook of nothing, not one morsel. Not one woman. All of the close or tender relationships were similarly played by Travelers. In time, out of time, you had to function as behind a wall. Only the forms mattered. Tender relationships. Tender sausage.

The woman said something in German that was incomprehensible to Reuter. The translator then *had* broken down. This was the second time this had happened to him. Working Carter in the old temple, he had found the soldiers staring at him, looking at one another with rising incomprehension, and it had been only by luck that the thing had cut in on him again; he might have lost the entire scene. Now this. Perhaps it was true what the rumors were about the Department, that it had so many enemies on certain levels of the Institute that technical malfunction was being deliberately induced by failure to replace equipment. You would not want to think this . . . you would not want to think of that kind of malevolence . . . but you had to encompass all of the possibilities. Certainly it was known that there were many who felt that the Department served no purpose whatsoever.

The woman repeated the same phrase, more loudly. Reuter gestured at the sausage, pointed to his ear, smiled, and shook his head. He would have to feign literal deafness, after all, in order to survive. Perhaps it would enhance the credibility of his role if he did so.

The woman shrugged and took out the sausage, cut

a small slice, put it into a brown wrapper, and gave
the whole mess to him. "Three marks," she said, as
Reuter perceived with relief that the translator had
begun to work again. Like him. Like his Traveling. Like
his life. He could not be sure that at odd moments he
would not lose control, but then again the moments
would be superseded and he would be able to go on
as if nothing had happened. Only up to a point, of course.
"What is wrong with you?" the woman said. "Are you
deaf? Are you crazy? Why are you standing there, not
listening to me and staring out the window? Are all of
you musicians crazy or do you simply not care as long
as you have your sausage?"

Crude, unidiomatic translation as usual. Little sophis-
tication in the devices. "No," Reuter said, fumbling in
his pocket, "I was merely thinking of something. Some
passage," he said, stricken with an idea, "some passage
in a symphony now in progress. You know that I am
a musician and often we have notes in our heads."

"That is not all you have in your heads. It would
well suit your purposes to listen, to attend to people.
You cannot in this world of ours listen to notes in your
head all the time, even at the King's pleasure."

"Of course," Reuter said. He handed the woman some
coins. One, two, three marks. By this time he should
be accustomed to transactions in strange tongues and
strange currencies, but he was not. He never had been.
He was perfectly able to work with the personae in
private. Even with Beethoven, for whom he felt no sympathy, he could at least *feel* the way the Heiligenstadt
Testament must have come out of him, but in a sausage
shop he could not believe that this was quite happening.
He had never believed what was happening, which was

one of the reasons—this occurred to him shockingly—
why the Board might be right after all. How could he
be a Traveler when at an important level he could not
take any of this seriously? Was it possible that he had
no faith in the existence of the Department itself?

"One of my very latest symphonies," he said wildly,
and he took the bag from the woman and left the shop.

The streets of Vienna overtook him in waves as he
lurched down them, and for just a moment he had a
brief intimation of Buenos Aires as it might be if super-
imposed upon this landscape: it would be larger but in
many ways it would contain Vienna without alteration
. . . and he found this thought as sickening as the smell
of rancid meat coming from the mess. Hurriedly he dis-
posed of it underneath an abandoned carriage, moving
back rapidly then to the security, such as it was, of his
rooms. The sacrifices a Traveler made. The sacrifices a
Traveler made in order that the currents of culture might
continue to run secure and full. In any case, they had
told him that. He simply did not know. He simply did
not know.

Well, so much for 1802 anyway, he thought. Finish
the Heiligenstadt episode and the next stop would be
the court and the Seventh Symphony. At least it was
not continuous; he could live Beethoven's life only in
little pieces. To live it continuously would have killed
him, he was now utterly convinced, as utterly as it would
have killed Beethoven. For real.

Andante moderato

The Department of Reconstruction had evolved from
the theories of Karl Kemper, a mad physicist of the

twenty-second century who, shortly after the invention of time travel, had posited that the very existence of the process proved that the past was flux and that it had to be eternally reconstructed by surrogates from the present, who would go back in time and live out key aspects in the lives of famed historical personages in order to make sure that the present did not dissolve.

Kemper had been discharged from the Lyceum of Berlin in 2159 for a series of disastrous experiments that had resulted in the death by explosion of five of his colleagues. He had been committed to the Pilgrimage four years later with what appeared to be a terminal schizophrenia beyond even the drug techniques of the time, but somehow he had emerged from the Pilgrimage to find a minor position in the Balkan Department of Physical Research. From there he had published his theories in small, disreputable journals.

The essence of his theories was that the present was only a speculation that had to be constantly reinforced. The invention of time travel itself proved that this was so, because time travel made it possible to relive and reconstruct the past, which possibility had to be fulfilled. The papers were written in vile Esperanto and struck most serious scholars in Kemper's field as being unreasoned and quite mad, but Kemper, by his own testimony, was writing eclectically and looking for a much larger audience.

Kemper's core speculation was that his theory could be proved true if the reconstruction of historical figures were evolved. He believed that upon the return of surrogates from the present to the past, it would be found that the surrogates were the actual personages, that there had been, in short, no JFK, Chamberwit, Thomas Alva

Guinzaburg other than those who were the surrogates. This would make clear, Kemper had postulated, that the past was an absolute creation of the present and that indeed it was only the concept of a timeless present, working toward both future and past, that sustained all of human existence.

Kemper had footnoted in his third paper his perfect willingness to withdraw his theories if, upon the enactment of a surrogate standard and a Department of Reconstruction, it was found that the surrogates were competing uncomfortably for attention with the absolute historical personages whom they were supposed to imitate. He had then, shortly after the publication of this final paper, killed himself in a fit of pique after being publicly denounced from the podium of the Interdisciplinary Council. The Council had seen fit in its annual conference to hold a seminar on Kemper's theories precisely to discourage their popular interest, because, due to the free-flux journalism of the time and the work of the itinerant but highly charismatic spiritualists of that era, the theories had been rather widely distributed and had excited a good deal of cult interest among the masses.

Kemper had deliberately choked to death upon an inhaled handful of thimbles, but his theories had held. The economics of that rather affluent and globally homogenized era had made the financing of a Department of Reconstruction for serious pursuit of Kemper's theories easier than dealing with the mass unrest that spiritualists might create by accusing the technocracy of deliberately risking all of human progress and existence. It was also to the interest of the technocracy to control and limit time travel, which might otherwise have passed into disparate private hands and been used for purposes less benevolent than Kemper's postulates. Some individuals, for instance, might return to the past in order to murder the ancestors of their enemies or, worse yet, threaten to do so unless tribute was paid.

Thirty-seven years after Kemper had turned a ghastly blue in his last attempts to expectorate seventeen pinky-sized thimbles, the first surrogates were sent back a cautious two hundred years to investigate the existence at that time of an English Prime Minister and a satellite-country dictator. It might have given Kemper great satisfaction to know that both surrogates returned with the astounding news that, garbed in the appropriate clothing of that time and placed in appropriate circumstances, they had filled the roles of the dictator and Prime Minister with exactitude, had in fact *been* the dictator and Prime Minister.

But then again it might have given Kemper no satisfaction whatsoever. He was a complex and bitter man, quite mad, of course, and he had also footnoted in his second paper that his theories, if true, had a tragic overcast. Humanity would not only be responsible for its future but for its past; it would have to evolve and reenact the past as carefully as it strove for the future, and with time telescoped as it was by necessity, the present would have to be of almost negligible significance. It might in fact turn out, Kemper had concluded, that human existence was so entirely deterministic that the present could not be said to exist in any other terms than the support it gave to past and future . . . a dismal prospect for a humanity that was just then beginning to break past Western mysticism and into an order of religion which held that for the most part the present was eternal, and one could, if one would, live forever by existing in that presence.

Nevertheless, the implications of the message delivered by the first two surrogates had been clear. If the past indeed was so open to receive them, then it had to be postulated that *all* of the past was open and that almost all of history had been enacted by carefully trained, conscientiously manipulative Travelers from the present.

The Department of Reconstruction at that time had enlarged enormously; from a staff of 350 (including all technicians) it had been brought by frantic, secretive crash programming to 47,000, half of whom were placed in training to be surrogates who would act out various key roles through the most recent five hundred years of history. Due to the lack of precise biographical details and precise, documented records of lives or appearances far into the past, it was arbitrarily decided to cut off the Department at the five-hundred-year waterline and hope for the best.

Within one year the first tentative journeys had been made and all of them yielded the same findings: the surrogates were the actual personages. JFK was a surrogate, so was Chopin. Ravel, Saint-Saëns, Nikita Khrushchev, Hitler, Napoleon Bonaparte, Prince von Metternich, Winston Churchill . . . every historical personage whose life was to be reenacted under the Kemper theories was reconstructed by the Travelers. (Working out a way to avoid public assassinations or, as in the case of Peter Ilich Tchaikovsky, a very public death from choleric poisoning for the Traveler, was difficult, but the Department had its resources and was aided to no small degree by its ability to make instant recall and precise delivery.

All of the critical events of human history, it was now theorized, had been carefully staged, acted out as with props and dumbshow, but as Kemper himself had noted in yet another of the footnotes to the papers, human life had always been known to be absurd; nothing could be said to compound an absurdity other than truth—of which, Kemper had concluded, there was very little at all.)

After these initial findings the Department became even more vastly enlarged, and its undertakings were taken with considerable seriousness. Of course paradoxologists had cause to note that the Department's existence might be an ultimate absurdity. If all that happened had already occurred, then the existence of the Travelers had already been postulated, and it made no difference exactly what role the Department played. But the paradoxologists had begun in low esteem, and only several decades later did their suggestions begin to be taken seriously and the Department fell into somewhat lower repute. It did begin to appear to the Institute that there was a very shaky basis for a subdivision whose sole purpose seemed to be to keep matters of the world exactly as they were, and whose efficacy could only be guessed.

Reuter had gone into the Department during this time of relative disrepute because it appeared to be interesting work and there were very few openings in more prestigious positions for members of his subclass. His original intention had been to be a Traveler for no more than one year, after which he would try to get transferred into another division, perhaps that of Resettlement and Slaughter, but now he had already been a Traveler for five years. The work was somehow hypnotic and yet mechanical. The range of actual choices for a Traveler was very narrow. Almost anything you did was all right as long as you kept to the basic forms. The same could be said of almost all existence, Reuter rationalized, so what?

So what!

Adagio

Reuter paused in 1809 to attend the first rehearsal of the Fifth Symphony and then was taken to a checkpoint. The musicians laughed at the strange sounds made by the opening four notes, then put down their instruments while Reuter, in frock coat, conferred with the conductor.

"It is a silly omen," the conductor said, "perhaps some rearrangement of the tempo might improve. You cannot blame the musicians; they are relatively unsophisticated folk, most of them, but then again discipline must be enforced. Perhaps you could consider a slow opening so that the theme would not sound quite so burlesque, so common, perhaps."

Reuter told him no, that his artistic convictions were absolute, that he knew precisely what effects he sought to obtain with the opening notes and that the conductor and musicians should follow the score with absolute accuracy, respect the composer's intention. What with the profound way in which the opening theme of the Fifth Symphony would penetrate human affairs for the next four centuries, it was impossible for Reuter to yield in any way, and yet once again he felt a tickle of impossibility, one of those surges of doubt that more and more had been interrupting his progress, and which the Board had noted. The Fifth was the Fifth, wasn't it? It had always been there; presumably it always would. The paradoxologists could well be right. Why should he go back to Vienna to be a silly, gnomish man eating liverwurst in a frock coat in order to sustain a reality that everyone knew to be completely objective? It was possible that the Department was wholly absurd, that it had no function at all. Kemper was mad; he was reenacting the obsessions of a madman.

Perhaps. Perhaps not. It was impossible to tell. One could only follow the dictates of Kemper, it was not the purpose of the Department to do otherwise. Reuter worked himself into a comic rage at the musicians, not knowing if it was rage at Kemper and the process, at himself, or at the musicians who, it had to be admitted—the truth had to be faced—were a sleazy and pathetic lot. Half of them appeared to be outright drunk; all of them seemed to have body odor. Of course Reuter knew quite well the status of musicians at this time, even those who played for the courts, but still. . . . Still.

There was no question, he could now see, as to why the arts had almost always had such hard going in the technological cultures that began at the beginning of the twentieth century: the arts were dirty, whereas technology was sterile and clean. Although he had little use for technology himself, he could well understand—Reuter would have been totally without perception if he had not understood—why art would have had hard going. The miracle was, indeed, that the Department found it as necessary to reconstruct the lives of people like Beethoven as it did the lives of Gregor Mendel or

Niels Bohr, but they were conscientious there, Reuter supposed. Highly conscientious. Either that or they subscribed to the belief that the world might indeed be held together by a feather; blow away the one and you might lose it all.

The musicians shook their heads, seemed otherwise detached during his tirade. Actually Reuter agreed with them; his musical ear might not be the soundest, but the musical phrase was, in its way, rather ridiculous. Somewhat ridiculous. The conductor, however, was not similarly detached. Indeed, he seemed to interpret his role as being as offensive to Reuter as possible. (It had long since crossed Reuter's mind, of course, that the conductor might be another Traveler. Many of the people with whom he had dealt on various assignments might have been surrogates. The Bureau would leave little to chance and was so compartmentalized that any given Traveler was aware of the appearance of only the twenty others in his own unit. The Department, having gone this far, would not be likely to slip up in checkable details. If history said that the musicians at the first rehearsal of the Fifth had laughed at the four-note motif and the conductor had been abusive, then the Department, history's delegate, would do everything within its power to serve the cause of history, Reuter supposed.)

"Do not abuse my many fine musicians," the conductor said in execrable translation, his eye acquiring a strange cast as if he were winking. But then again he might not be. "My musicians work hard and with extreme difficulty in order to rise to performance levels. They should not be subjected to abuse."

"The motif is of the greatest importance," Reuter said.

"It reappears at key points not only throughout the first movement but once again in the finale. To laugh at it is to fail of comprehension."

"It is not to fail of comprehension," the conductor said, and Reuter was sure now that he *was* winking. There was a collaborative whiff in the air; even the musicians seemed to be giving one another grins. Was there no past? Were they all in this together, collaborating on a past, or was this merely another symptom of his increasing alienation? "The performer's right to the work is as sacred as the creator's, and the performer has a right to his own expression."

"I have a right to my feelings," Reuter said. Was this actually happening in Vienna in 1808? In some strange way, he thought, it might be going on in the complex; perhaps the past was an illusion. Perhaps there was no past at all; perhaps the Department had lied to them, and they were not being carried back toward the past but were being induced to believe that while actually, with the help of certain hypnotics, they were reenacting with one another in safe dioramas which had constructed their own version of the past for their own benefit. Then again . . . you could not be sure of anything.

"An absolute right to my feelings," he said, and felt the revulsion beginning to build. They were right—the Board was right—in what they had said to him; he simply was unable to sustain his belief in this at some crucial level. He was not sure that any of this was going on and he was losing conviction. His stutter was not Beethoven; his posture reminded him of the old, familiar, ruined Reuter who had come to the Department some time ago and begged for employment.

"Just do as you must," he said, trying to stay within

the role. "Do all as must be done. Do absolutely the right, but do not mock my work. Respect my work; it is, after all, all that I have. It is by that I will be judged if I will be judged by anything at all."

Peculiar. A good exit line. He had always had the sense of them—within the rigid limits of the programming he had found some excellent captions in his time—and yet, as he turned, in what seemed to be a curiously airless space, it was as if the line, the situation itself, worked against him. His own facility was somewhat humiliating, he thought; his ability to control situations, to back away from them somehow, as he had from this, and see himself functioning within a role, somehow drained the situations of meaning, made him wonder about the purpose of his life. If he was unable to take Beethoven seriously, was it possible then that Beethoven was somehow a comic figure and his life and works would have to be subsequently judged at a reduced scale? He did not know, of course, he simply did not know; speculations of this nature were supposed to fall utterly outside the functioning of the Travelers.

He turned and left the hall. Behind him he could hear the chattering of the musicians, the thin sound of a single bow scraping against an E string as someone mocked the four-note pattern. Scurrilous: these people had no respect. Outside, in the dirty street, he saw the transfer booth waiting for him behind an abandoned peddler's cart laden with merchandise so odorous that pedestrians moved away from it. They were so clever. Their arrangements were exquisite; you could always count on the Department to act with foresight.

He moved toward it with fair haste, was almost struck on the head by a flying sausage thrown from far above, felt the sausage glance from his shoulder, staggered gracelessly into the booth. Instantly the darkness closed over him and, clutching it as if it were real, he felt himself, in tumult, moved.

Presto

Roughly his clothes were taken from him, he was laved by a corps of disinterested, efficient attendants. The gleaming bowl of the retention quarters had never seemed more threatening to him; he had to be deeply in the Beethoven persona to be this offended by sterility. New clothing was given him, the attendants muttered requisite assurances into his ear, and he was whisked on a rotating table—no reason to let him touch anything in quarters inasmuch as he would soon be back in Vienna—into a room where the Supervisor waited, holding a sheaf of papers in his hand.

It was the same Supervisor as at the last checkpoint after 1798, when his career as a soloist had gone down the drain, but that was of no significance. Nothing of that sort had any significance. You could have the same Supervisor for three or four checkpoints, even for a whole reconstruction, and then the next time around you could have four or five different ones. Once you flung yourself to the mercy of the Department and assumed that their procedures had nothing to do with the individual assignment, you were on the first step of the way toward being a real Traveler. At least that was what had been made clear throughout the orientation seminars. *Trust us as we trust you. We know what is best.*

"You're overacting a little," the Supervisor said, "also

showing too much stress. Sometimes you are coming out of the role."

"The deafness," Reuter explained, "shattering psychic effect; after all, to a composer—"

"Nevertheless. The texts are very clear on this point; there was some self-pity but also much fortitude. Self-pity and heroism, these were the only two moods of the subject. You must be able to call upon one or the other or a blend, but not move beyond. Also, you are overdoing some of the eccentricities. There was diet other than sausage."

"Very well."

"In some ways your work is quite satisfactory. The outburst to the orchestra was quite neatly conceived."

"I knew it was in character."

"It is important, however, that there be a sense of total conviction. You cannot lapse. We are dealing, after all, with a central historical figure, the cornerstone, so to speak, of modern music. The five piano concerti, the ten symphonies—"

"Nine symphonies."

"*Come?*"

"He wrote nine symphonies, not ten."

"Oh," the Supervisor said. "Well, no difference." He consulted some papers in his hand. "Perfectly true; there were only nine symphonies."

"He died with some notes for a tenth, but they were lost, or at least appropriated by someone."

"Quite so," the Supervisor said. "On balance, your performance is adequate, however. There are elements of real range and passion. If you could open up some more levels of pain—"

"I don't understand how you could think there were *ten* symphonies," Reuter said. "There were nine, that's a very common fact."

"No difference. That's your specialty. Now, when I talk about pain, I mean—"

"It's not a matter of specialty. It's just something that you ought to know. I mean, if you're reconstructing the past, then it should be assumed that you know the details you're seeking to reconstruct. Wouldn't that be reasonable?"

The Supervisor shook his head. Reuter had always had difficulty in individuating technocratic types; nevertheless, he was forming a very strong impression of this one. It was as if, coming back in this persona, he was open as never before to appearances, implications. The Supervisor was a man very much like the conductor in Vienna; he appeared to be drained of feeling. But then again perhaps Reuter was overreacting.

"Creative anguish," the Supervisor said, "and its carry-over into the processes of everyday living. The matter of the unrequited entanglements, the unconnected search for love. There is very little time," he said. "You'll have to be prepared for reentry now. But I hope that you will keep all of this in mind."

"You want pain," Reuter said. "That's what you're saying. Pain and ten symphonies."

"Only nine. Strict adherence to historical fact, of course."

"Not one or the other, but both."

"Exactly."

"Historical accuracy and pain."

"Precisely."

"They are the same," Reuter said, stricken with insight. "They are exactly the same; that is what Kemper must have been really trying to tell us." His readings on Kemper were very shaky, just as was the case with all the Travelers, who were conceived of as technicians, not theoreticians, but even with his very shaky, superficial understanding of what Kemper had been saying, Reuter nevertheless felt himself coming close to something very important: history as pain. Kemper felt that one had to relive the pain over and over again if one was even to retain custody of the present, let alone make way for the future—pain and pain reenacted over all the generations and in all guises. The insight made him gasp, it was all so complete, it came together so thoroughly.

But then they quickly came to take him out of there, the Supervisor looking at him in a detached way, the attendants not without concern as they put him into a fresh set of clothes and threw him into the bewildering Vienna of 1823, all alone again but for his memories of the Immortal Beloved, his ambivalent longings for his nephew Karl and, of course, his pain. His pain, his pain, his pain, his pain.

Allegro ma non troppo

They skipped around, of course. A Traveler's job was not to fathom their methods. You might take six months in subjective time and then find yourself dropped in at widely separated one-day slots down the line. It was as if history were in constant revision of emphasis. Then again there were rumors—but none of the Travelers was sure—that different surrogates occupied the persona at different stages of his life so that they had an entire range of skills, each of them best equipped for the moments that they lived. You were best off not thinking about that. You were simply best off taking the instructions, becoming acclimated to the surroundings, and doing the best you could on the level where you found yourself rather than being concerned with the workings of the Department or, for that matter, even the ultimate significance of your role.

Kemper had postulated life as meaningless, existing in present time only for the purpose of reconstructing itself. The Supervisor had thought that he had written ten symphonies, not concluding with the immortal Ninth. Dealing with such people, you were better off not dealing with yourself, but just trying to do the job.

He tried to do the job. New rooms in Vienna in 1823, but otherwise the same city, the same landscape, the same poisonous, strictured roadways, and tumult. Little visible progress had been made in a decade and a half; human life in many ways was in utter stasis until the time of the industrial revolution.

Reuter could feel the deterioriation in his body, however. By that alone he could measure the gap: the deafness was now absolute, and he seemed to have a series of small warts and pockmarks working their way not only into the crevices of his features but up and down his limbs. He certainly was a rather disgusting specimen physically; there was no mystery about why the Immortal Beloved, whoever she was, would have nothing to do with him. Reuter could hardly bear to have much to do with himself. Within the short, gross frame he could feel the small, coursing damages of age carried by the ruined blood; he could feel the breakdown of the organism being carried in every shattered, uneven breath that he drew as he hunched over the desk, working on the final draft of the Ninth Symphony.

The price paid for being Beethoven was certainly high, but no higher than what the Department was exacting from him, piece by piece, every moment of his life, Reuter thought, and it was at that moment, carefully working in the transposition of the opening themes so that the fifths bridged of D moll into the key of B, that he realized this would be his last assignment. He simply could not take this any more. The price that was being exacted from him was more than he could pay. None of his other roles had been like this. Minor politicians mostly, Talleyrand once, in the arts only the painter Marc Putnam, but that hardly counted as an artist. Putnam was a drunk with one significant canvas.

Beethoven had been significant for him, a breakthrough, his first major assignment, his first time to put his musical interests, augmented by the hypnotics, to credible use, but he had never had to deal with a persona like this before. The pain was constant now. The fifty-three-year-old Beethoven was a man in agony; emotional waste and poor hygiene had broken him down completely. To say nothing of the creative process. In being inside this persona it was as if Reuter for the first time were beginning to apprehend his own life: it was a pretty sorry fix. It was a pretty sorry fix indeed if it would lead him to having to do something like this.

"Uncle," someone said from the corner.

Reuter turned abruptly, shaking with fear, and saw a young man sitting on the piano bench before the open keyboard (the piano in the room was a new touch since 1803; matters must have slightly improved for him over these years. He realized then that of course this was Karl, would have to be Karl. Who else would be sitting in his odorous dark rooms and calling him Uncle in 1823? Certainly not the Supervisor.

"You should out some air and go to public, Uncle. It is for health bad to sit in depression such Uncle."

Translation failure again. Why hadn't he brought it up with the Supervisor, mentioned that the devices did not seem to be working properly during this reconstruction? Well, he should have, but instead he had listened to a lot of garbage about ten symphonies and passion. That was the problem with the Department—they were not, for all their rhetoric, very efficient at all. Little got done. "I a major symphonic entrance am concluding," he heard himself say. "Outside in the air is symphonies not."

"Accompany me not Uncle then?"

"No," he said in execrable translation, "remain with one's work I must. It source and savior of life is, and manuscript is owed and due as well on commission firm."

"Then droshmarks gibben me, Uncle," Karl said, and stood, walked over to him.

Gibben me? Next the machine would begin to spew Chinese. Karl certainly was an awkward young man. Reuter could hardly comprehend, looking at him closely, way there were rumors of a homosexual attachment, if not direct commission, between subject and nephew. He was much taller than Reuter, of course, perhaps five nine, which in these times was considered an outstanding height, but then again his features were coarse and uneven, and even through the abominable translator he could catch the suggestion of a lisp. There was something effeminate and duplicitous in his bearing, too: Karl was obviously a youth who could not be trusted. Still, there was no accounting for the taste. What you had to do was to accept the life of the subject, not try to change it. Reuter knew that well; it was one of the first tenets of the training; he knew it as well as he had ever known anything in his life, but he had a strong urge to punch Karl in the face and run screaming from the room.

"I do not to you wish droshmarks give," he said sullenly. "Droshmarks earning in this world is gifts are not."

"Uncle then gibben," Karl said, and put out his hand. His features suddenly became suffused with light, as if they were catching a stray beam darting through the window. Reuter began to understand the hold the youth might have had, after all. It *was* a rather charming smile. Too, there was so little in his life, it was a kind of contact. . . .

"Here," he said, going into his pocket, finding the money, which had been thoughtfully supplied (the small cosmetic details were always taken care of). "Here some droshmarks gibben is. You will to me explaineth the sources on your return of pleasure." *Explaineth?*

"Uncle, gibben is as gibben does," Karl said sincerely and took the money *flick!* as quickly as the Transporters whisking Reuter into checkpoint. Then he turned, moved rapidly toward the door of the room, turned at the door, bestowed upon Reuter the most fleeting of smiles, and went out briskly, the ratcheting sound of his feet on the stairs somehow reminding Reuter of the pelting rhythms of the Seventh. The Seventh? He must have worked on that over a decade ago, objective time. Strange that it should be so vivid in his mind now. Of course it had been only a couple of hours subjectively since the first rehearsal of the Fifth. Images enjamb. Life contracts.

Reuter tried to apply himself to the work, but it was not easy. Many things were disturbing him now, and another insight was also growing. It might be the central insight. He really had no particular affection for music.

Allegro assai

It was amazing really how little human contact the Travelers had between assignments. (It was amazing how little human contact they had *on* assignments, but that was another level of complaint entirely.) Once Reuter had been bitter; he had somehow envisioned that coming out of the underclass to the rather glamorized conception he had had of the Department he would, if nothing else, meet any number of interesting people in similar circumstances and have a number of fascinating relationships. This had not occurred. He had, rather, found that he lived insulated and alone. Assignments left little latitude for contact, of course; it was all so controlled and the changes so abrupt that it was hard to sink into any kind of relationship. Away from their duties, Travelers had just as little to do with one another, living in sector quarters in their separate cubicles and keeping largely to themselves. The Department did not disapprove of Travelers' having relationships, not exactly, but in effect relationships were not possible. The job was so exacting, for one thing, and for another so much was given to the roles that there was little enough outside of them. Reuter knew that most of the time, at rest, he had no sense of himself. Also, Travelers had to be rather superficial, rootless people in order to fulfill their function. If they had had a strong persona or real sense of identity, they would not have been drawn to the Department in the first place. So the fact was that their isolation from one another, like their isolation from themselves, was almost complete.

Reuter had had a couple of fumbling relationships here, a little bit of something more serious there, but all of this had been at the beginning, when he had been relatively fresh and naive and had entered relationships without expectations and without the demoralizing factors involved in playing various roles. Coming from the underclass to the Department had been initially liberating; he had felt that whole vistas of experience were opening up, and at least at the beginning he had thought that he was finding some. But now he knew that to be a Traveler was to engage in a reduction of experience.

Although this made him bitter when he thought about it, most of the time he did not think about it at all. He did very little thinking. The periods between assignments were for recuperation and then for study; two weeks off and then the hypnotics would begin again. Two weeks of hypnotics and briefing and into the past. Two weeks of subjective time in the past and then back for recuperation. It was a difficult life, but then again, as Kemper had pointed out in yet another of his footnotes (Kemper saved his best insights for footnoting; the main texts of his work were written in a dull, virtually impenetrable prose), the life of the Surrogates would have to be sacrificial. Only at the altar of history, kneeling, could one infer present time.

Part of Reuter's failure to find relationships with his fellows (he thought about this occasionally) might have to do with the general impoverishment of emotional life that came from being part of the underclass. It was—he had a little perspective on his life and could now understand—a matter of living outside of the complexes, so close to the actual physical necessities, the raw stuff of life, so to speak, that an emotional life was a relative luxury. Once you came into the complexes, even if only as a member of the Department, you had that pressure taken from you, perhaps for the first time in your life, and could acquire a more detached perspective. But then, too, the first decades of your life might have inflicted such enormous emotional damages that, even given opportunities now, you could not change.

Which was why, to the extent that he could be said to live at all, Reuter was beginning to understand, he might live only as a Traveler. In the reconstitution of role. In the bowels of an imaginary past being built piece by slow piece in order that five hundred years later he might be given—

Exactly what he had now.

There was an irony in that, but perhaps he was too emotionally impoverished, he thought, to appreciate it.

Presto

Quickly the soloist spoke to him. "These passages are impossible," the contralto said. "They cannot be sung. The octaves, the rhythms are beyond breath."

The chorus, up in racks behind them, and the orchestra murmured. Someone applauded.

"Really," the contralto added, "you have got to have some consideration for the limitations of the human voice, Maestro."

At least the translator was back to working properly. Jiggling around at range, they had probably found the right splices at last. Always working, you could give the technicians that. The Travelers might have their limitations, but the Department, necessarily, had the best technicians available.

"I agree," the tenor added. "At least some bridging passages should be inserted."

"That is absolutely true," the bass said quickly. "I am a full octave above my own staff."

"Indeed," the soprano added rapidly, "I think that it has been spoken for all of us, Maestro. The work is one of supreme difficulty; it is unperformable."

Reuter looked away from the quartet, looked at the chorus above him, looked at the orchestra, at the little conductor, who was twisting his baton between somewhat misshapen hands. Another surrogate? He did not look like any conductor to him. Maybe they were all surrogates. Maybe unknowingly they were reconstructing a past that had never existed for a future that did not need it all because Kemper was crazy. Kemper had created all of this pain for illusion.

Of course he was very tired. He was close to an edge of neurasthenic exhaustion, which he had never apprehended in any of his previous roles. Then again, he had never had to be a Beethoven before.

"You will perform it as written," he said.

"But we cannot," the contralto said. She was a large, aggressive woman, probably the leader of this revolt. Then again, perhaps they had put her up to it. You never could be sure with people. Human motivations, past or present, were tangled, poisonous: a bloody network. "We cannot."

"Emendations should be made," the conductor said.

The chorus applauded lightly. "Reasonable small cuts, perhaps a transposition—"

"No."

"We have found in the early rehearsals that many of the choral passages do not work."

"They will work."

"They are too *high*, Maestro."

"Too low," the bass said.

"Too much bridging," said the tenor, "too many leaps."

"And the violins in the final presto," the concertmaster said, "these passages are totally out of their means and I must make an objection—"

"There are many objections," the conductor said. "One must come to grips, shake life by the throat, so to speak, and we must make demands, the performer's right to—"

"No," Reuter said loudly. "No, no, there will be no changes!" Rage filled him, his own pure rage, fused with persona. "The work is one of absolute integrity; it is my masterwork, perhaps the greatest piece of music ever written, it will not be abominated by incompetents! The work is the central vision of my entire life. Of course the last quartets can be said to break through into newer and stranger ground, a more profound, spiritual vision, as it were, but then again they are limited work, work done on quite a reduced scale, and will have a much smaller, more specialized audience. No, it is proper to say that it is the Ninth that will live and live. Performance standards are well within your means; by the twentieth century the work will fall well into the range of any modestly competent orchestra and singers. Indeed, it will be approached with pleasure by the soloists, who will look for it to be a tour de force, an opportunity to exercise their full range of skills. The work will be popular and central to the repertory, it will be much in demand and will please everyone almost every time. You cannot imagine how low your own performance standards are, compared as to how they will be in a mere seventy-five years. Why, the great and demanding works of Richard Wagner—"

He paused. Was it possible that he was saying this? Could he bring witness to his own speech? Was it conceivable that he was actually doing this thing? He was breaking one of the central directives of the Department; he was rupturing the integrity of the past, breaking that contained bubble of time so that waters were rushing here and there, backward and forward. He was literally exploding the past, bringing to it anachronism, and that was the one thing that no Traveler could do, the single most dangerous thing.

And yet he was so tired. He was so tired. First, there had been fear and then there was pain and now at last, with Beethoven, he seemed to have gone to the farthest edge of the emotional spectrum. He was tired, and with it had come an absolute loss of control.

Conductor, soloists, chorus, orchestra peered at him incomprehendingly. Was it possible that the translator had broken down? No, no such luck; precisely when it would be useful to have malfunction, it would work. It would work. Perversity of technology. What was he doing? What was he doing? How could this have happened to him?

Reuter spread his hands helplessly, felt phlegm rising from his chest, expectorated it noisily onto the floor, rubbed it with a shoe. Artistic eccentricity. "Do not mind," he said, "do not pay any attention to all of this. It is merely an outcome of my rather extreme exhaustion. It is wild talk. Foolishness."

"It is," the conductor said. "It is extremely foolish talk. Dangerous talk as well."

"I will return to my rooms to rest," Reuter said, "I will attend no further rehearsals."

"That would be extremely advisable," the conductor said, "I should think you would want to return to your rooms at once."

Reuter looked at the man. In the eyes now he could see no doubt, no indecision. It was as he had known; the conductor was a Traveler too, and as he cast his eyes upward toward the chorus, orchestra, soloists, he felt that the way in which they looked at him was drenching him with implicatory stain, stain that filled his glance, stain that filled all of the past, all of the mad world, and he turned as he had turned so many times before from confrontation and ran up the aisle then and into the widely strewn and distant network of Vienna.

Allegro assai

And you, too? he wanted to say to Karl, who was waiting for him in his rooms. *And you too, are you also one of them, are all of us merely part of the one great reconstruction, and in that case what is the past?*

But he did not, he did not; he was a reasonable man, always had been, had carried forth his assignments with great discipline and restraint. If there was one thing that could be said of him, it was that his discipline was enormous; the personae were absolute. At no time whatsoever had his real personality peeked through the shroud of those whom he was reconstructing. Once maybe—all right, twice—a couple of the incidents with Beethoven might have been overacting due to stress, but even then he had been essentially true to the character. Of course. Of course he had. Even now, when for the first time he was beginning to understand the gigantic fraud that the Department had perpetrated, was still perpetrating upon them, even now, he was beginning to understand that his discipline was absolute.

"I want you out of these rooms," he said to Karl. "I want you out at once."

"Uncle—"

"Out!" he said, and waved a small, wart-pocked, swarthy arm. "I want you out now!" He bore down upon his nephew threateningly and thought that he saw an instant's true distress pass across Karl's features, but then it was gone and Karl was into himself, contained, just as he had always been.

"You are very disturbed, Uncle," Karl said. "I do not understand the source of your disturbance, but if you would prefer me to leave—"

"I would prefer you to leave," he said. "I would prefer you to leave." And Karl stood, shook his head, assembled his garments quickly, and backed toward the door, Reuter pursuing him. "Now," he said. "I can no longer deal with it; I want you out of here now." And Karl was at the door, reaching behind him. "Go," he said, seized by a complex of emotions that he had never felt in a role before. This must be one of the consequences of feeling truly, deeply, and if nothing else he was now possessed of feeling, he could no longer shield himself. If there was no past, if it was all a dream of the present reconverted, then there was no way in which feeling should be denied—nor could it be denied.

"Go!" he said, and Karl reached toward him the shyest and most tentative of palms. He felt the tentative touch of the youth upon his cheek, and it was a shock, flesh against flesh, carrying him to some confrontation he could not bear. He might have struck him then, might have struck Karl violently, but the youth turned and went out, leaving the door open, clattering down the stairs just as he had the first time.

And he is my *collaborator,* Reuter thought. He is doing this exactly in this way in order to help me, in order to *perpetuate the scene.* All the time he had thought that he had been moving alone through all of the interstices of history, but he had been wrong. He had been only one of many; all of them were collaborators. The past existed only as that open maw through which all of them, descended, could scramble together. The thought was horrifying. It was a horrifying thought because, if it was true, the past was purely speculative, in the process of merely being another aspect of history.

His pain shifted, went to another level. If that was true, he could hardly be said to exist. He existed only in terms of the demands of a past that had had no shape. Now there was a thought—there was a thought that could inspire some last quartets. There was a thought that could send a composer to his writing table to produce those terrible mysteries of anguish ascendant. Not that he wanted to do any writing now, not that composition fell anywhere within his level of intention. But here was another thought—here was another thought. Now Reuter felt himself being lifted to a high plain of circumstance where insights came battering upon him like thunder.

Like Prometheus chained to his rock shaking his fist at Olympus, he raised his hand against the heavens. Now there was melodramatics for you! But at last he had a good understanding of the character. No wonder Beethoven was self-pitying. But still the insight came pouring in—no way to avoid it now. Now, granted all that had happened, how could it be that—

Vivace

He was deaf and was still able to engage in dialogues with Karl, conductor, soloists, orchestra. *How could he be deaf and still conduct normal conversations?* The anachronism was overwhelming. Why had he never thought of it before? Why had this never occurred to him? What could be wrong with him if he had failed to question this?

Reuter felt his senses begin to reel. All right, that was a melodramatic phrase too, but everything was a melodrama—life was melodrama; it simply made no sense. None of it made any sense. How could the past be said to work if a deaf man could hear?

Reuter felt insight, like pain, beginning to batter at him, working up and down all the levels of his consciousness; circumstance burst within him like fire. "No sense!" he shouted. "It doesn't make any sense, none of it!" And he felt himself being seized as if by huge hands and being taken out of there. Here was salvation for you! The Department must have heard his cry in his hour of need, for he felt himself being lifted out of the room with amazing speed, and then he was in an enclosure, with cold around him, the icy surfaces of the room coming in close, and he looked up. He did not know

what he would see, he simply did not know what to
expect, but it was the familiar form of—

Alla marcia

The Supervisor saying, "You must be calm. You are
almost at the end of the cycle now. It is time to hold
on, to work through completion. You have not very far
to go now, you must be reasonable."

"It doesn't work," Reuter said. "Don't you understand
that? It isn't working, it isn't working. I can't believe
it anymore." The background of the room was gray—he
was drenched in gray. There was an absence of feature,
just, he thought, as had been in all the rooms of his
life with the exception of those pockets of the past in
which time and again he had enacted . . . well, what?
What had he enacted? Exactly what had it come to,
what did it mean? "It is a dream," he said, "all of it.
It has no reality."

"That is not true. That is not exactly true."

"You lied," Reuter said. He realized that he was lying,
strapped somewhere on a table, with small loops around
his wrists and ankles. He struggled toward confrontation,
but the straps held firm. Everything held firm—that was
always the point. That was the point you tried to evade
again and again, but eventually you had to confront it,
to accept the truth: they had you strapped in. "All of
you lied to us. How can this be the past if it makes
no sense?"

"Human life is senseless."

"That is no answer."

"That is the complete answer," the Supervisor said.

"In order to reconstitute senselessness, we must, time and again, enact it. That is all."

"That cannot be all," Reuter said. "There has to be more to it than this."

"There is. There are the ten symphonies."

"Nine. There are nine symphonies. There were never ten, only a series of notes—"

"The same," the Supervisor said, "it is all the same. It makes little difference."

"Ignorant," Reuter said, thrashing. "All of you are ignorant. You are as ignorant as I was."

"You are learning. We will learn."

"Enough," he said, "enough. Let me be free. Let it be done. I can go no further."

"You will have to finish this cycle. There is no alternative. Once you are in the cycle, you must work all of it through until completion. That is the most inflexible rule of the Department."

"Lies," Reuter said weakly. "All of it now, all of it was lies."

"To a higher purpose."

"We dreamed the past. It never existed."

"In the dreaming we made it real."

"We lived in deceit. All of it. Nothing ever existed."

"*This* exists," the Supervisor said. "The Department exists. You exist. I exist. We are real. You must hold on to the realities that you have. That is the only thing we can learn. The past is abstract."

"No," Reuter said. "I do not believe that. If the past is not real, then we have no existence. If we cannot believe in the past, what can we believe in?" He would have liked to continue this argument, really continue it, work

it through on all of the levels of discussion it truly deserved, but there was no way, no way at all. He felt
himself once again turning, being launched through time
or, then again, being launched through the present into
that abstraction, time, and found himself—

Andante maestoso

Present at the premiere of the Ninth Symphony. It
must have been the premiere because he was sitting on
the stage behind the orchestra, jammed between two
double basses. The orchestra was stumbling through the
introduction to the fourth movement as he sat there,
the score draped across his knees, beating a wild and
erratic time. This is the way it was supposed to have
been, according to all the texts; he was merely reconstructing them. A servant of bibliography, he thought.

It was hot in the hall, unbearably hot. Beyond the
orchestra he had a vague impression of audience, heat,
eaves, heat, and distraction, but his perspective had
narrowed to the score and the groaning of the contrabass.
He was trapped in the underside of his own symphony.

I am going to faint, Reuter thought, I am going to
faint on this stage. But of course he knew that he was
not—no such luck. He was doomed to full consciousness
throughout the range of the reconstruction. Nothing
would be denied him. He could not even move. It was
impossible to leave from this position; he might have
created a scandal leaving during the first performance
of his last symphony—what would they make of it?—and
then too he had to see it through to the end. They were
right. They were right at least in that insight: whatever
happened, you had to see it through to an end. In this

world or out of it, there were simply no choices. There
had never been choices; that was the illusion that was
given, but ultimately you were in your one pocket of
time and could only carry, carry, carry.

Burdened with more than he felt equipped to understand, Reuter nevertheless fluttered his hands, beat time,
beat time as the first notes of the choral theme came
muttering out of the contrabass, understanding at last—
but then again he must have always understood—that
he lived not in a continuum but in a reservoir and there
was no way out.

Allegro energico

He imagined himself to be having an interview with
the mad Karl Kemper. Maybe he was not imagining
Kemper at all; history was a closed unit embracing all
possibility. Why not, then, Kemper?

"Energetically," Kemper said to him, brushing some
crumbs from his beard. He was standing against a wall
in some amorphous room and eating a liverwurst sandwich on a roll, taking small bites and shaking his head,
as if the bites were sensual. Well, you knew physicists,
let alone Kemper. All of them were mad. "You must
reconstruct the past with energy, with conviction."

"But listen here," Reuter said, happy at last to have
the opportunity to put the case to the Founder, "it is
all a closed system. It exists only because of our presump-
tions. What does it matter how we do it?"

"It matters," Kemper said. "It matters. The attitude
must be one of utter conviction. Also, life is an energetic
business, counterforce as it is to the forces of entropy.
Why, life, my young man, is an aberration in the uni-

verse; it exists only by coincidence in a circumstance that was meant to be wholly dead. So it must be lived with passion, with conviction."

"I don't understand," Reuter said, but perhaps he did. Kemper had a very convincing way about him, and then the liverwurst sandwich was absolutely odorous, filling the room with little waves of smell; you could hardly minimize the accomplishments or veracity of a man who could eat a liverwurst sandwich like that. "What is, was; what was, is. We carry the attitude only inside ourselves. It does not matter."

"But of course it matters!" Kemper said, and flung the remains of the sandwich against a wall, watched while little crumbs and pieces of meat exploded in a shower of dust. "Life, being the only alternative, is sacred. We live, we create, we recreate sacred ground. To do otherwise is preposterous. Ah," Kemper said, "you are very young. You are very young still. You have not been dead as have I for two hundred years. Perhaps when you have had my experience, you will understand a little better. In the meantime," he concluded, "my time here is almost up, and I am afraid that we cannot continue our discussion. Perhaps some other time. Live with energy, feel with passion, give to the past what you know of the present in order that the future may be avoided. The future is total breakdown, you know. Good-bye, son. I would like to continue this at length sometime, but I have my own commitments to fulfill, and it is no easier for me, you must understand, than it is for you." And saying this, Kemper blossomed to enormous, vaporous size, seemed to tenant the entire room, and then vanished, oozing out of the crevices and leaving Reuter alone again.

How interesting, Reuter thought, how very interesting. It was a hallucinatory phenomenon on one level, of course, but on another, it was not. There were no hallucinations. That was what he had learned now. Everything was real. Everything that you touched was real. Knowing that, accordingly, Reuter seized life by the throat and—

Sempre ben marcato

Took himself to the boudoir of the Immortal Beloved, who was of course (as most historians had long since deduced) the Countess von Meck. She was not as compellingly attractive as the romanticized accounts of later times had indicated, but then the Vienna of that time was not populated by attractive figures, at least not by contemporary standards, and you had to allow a little romance to enter into the scheme. Without romance, where were you? Without a shade of sentiment, how could you go on? Even entropy had to flex, now and then, to a certain retrospective falsification.

"You will allow me to plight my troth," Reuter said with determination as the Countess, a large woman with a determined chin, looked at him patronizingly. "I have always been in love with you. You will inspire many of my most major works. Under those circumstances I see nothing to do but to propose an honorable marriage. Will you marry me? This unrequited love, after all, is a phenomenon of a different time."

"I am sorry," the Countess said, "I cannot possibly marry you." She seemed to have a little mad twinkle in her eyes. Well, by contemporary standards, most of ninteenth-century Vienna had also been insane. "I never did, therefore I cannot. I am sorry about that, of course, because in many ways you amuse me. You are a rather amusing, if trivial, person."

"We reconstruct the past. You can marry me if you will. If you do, you always did. Don't you understand?"

"I'm sorry," the Countess said with enormous sympathy. "I do understand your problem, to say nothing of unrequited love, but what was not, cannot be. Will you please leave my chambers now? I have to entertain several Lords for dinner, to say nothing of the scions of the great Metternich dynasty. I really move in very distinguished circles, you know; I'm afraid that, compared to them, you are in a totally disreputable trade—a juggler, a court musician."

"But you don't understand," Reuter said again. "You can do anything you want to do."

"Quite right," the Countess said determinedly. She stood and smoothed her skirts, looming over him, an imposing woman in many ways. "But even though we have limitless option, I still do not choose to do it. Free will exists in a vacuum, too; in a vacuum, free will is all we have. Get out of here, you ridiculous little man, before I summon the servants and have you physically thrown out of my boudoir."

"All right," Reuter said, "all right. I'll do that, but you'll pay for this. You'll pay for your errors. You'll regret it. You'll regret it every day of your life as long as you live."

"Regret is part of the process of living," the Countess said, and Reuter nodded. He could see the truth of that; there was much to be said for that way of looking at matters. For another thing, Kemper had never incorpo-

rated the concept of regret into his insights, which was
what you could expect from a man who ate liverwurst
sandwiches, of course. But on you went, on you went;
you did the best you could, and he—

Allegro ma non tanto

Skipped over Vienna, where the final great "Choral"
was beginning (everything in Vienna was under control—or out of control, depending upon how you looked
at it), and went instead directly to 1779 where, nine years
old, he confronted his father, a swarthy, neurotic man
with punishing hands and a vile temper. "No piano,"
he said, "no composition. I will not perform anymore.
I am unhappy being the instrument of your greed. I
abandon music."

"You will practice and perform!" his father said,
reaching out a punishing hand to seize him by the collar.

But Reuter in Beethoven's nine-year-old frame was
agile and cunning and slipped the terrible grasp. "No,"
he said, "no. I renounce, I refuse, I will not have any
part of this at all. I wish to live in feeling, not in art.
They are not the same. They are not the same thing
at all."

His father, a strong and vengeful man consumed by
torment, reached toward Reuter to shake him, then
lunged frantically, committing himself in one direction.
Expertly Reuter backed off, positioned himself, and lev-
eled a deadly kick to his father's jaw, breaking it in
three places and putting him into a dispensary in Munich
where in various ways the course of the present was
utterly changed. Then all existence fused within him and

he willed himself out of there, thinking that he might take another look at Vienna before his last and most vital performance. But he was interrupted by—

Poco adagio

The great machines of the Department, which plucked him out of there and deposited him struggling before the Directors. There were many of them now, and they seemed exceedingly grim. "Don't you see what you are doing?" one of them said. "This is dangerous, terrible."

"I am doing the necessary. I am at last controlling the flow of life."

"Craziness. This is craziness. You are to desist at once. You are to return to Vienna."

"I can do what I will," Reuter said. "You cannot stop me. None of you could ever stop me—that was my mistake from the outset. It was my assumption that I was in your control, but it was the other way. All of the time it was the other way. You cannot stop me."

"Why? Why are you doing this?"

"Under the dictates of Kemper," Reuter said. "I am finally doing what Kemper always wanted done. The past was not to be reconstructed; the past was to be lived. We can make of it anything we desire. We can make of ourselves anything we desire. It was always that way. That was the message that was struggling to break free from all of the researches, but you tried to hold it back. No more," Reuter said, "no more." He was enjoying the melodramatics of his posturing (very much in role), but thinking: This is true, all of this is true. It is an excellent point, but nevertheless I could not get the Immortal Beloved to marry me. If I could not get her to do that, there are questions that even Kemper, perhaps, could not answer. "Let me be," he said. "Let me finish the cycle. Let me lead my life. Live your own lives. All time is individual."

"You will destroy everything."

"I will destroy nothing. We live in a dream. All of this is a dream, a construction. The only reality is what we construct, piece by piece, our own way. Good-bye," Reuter said. "I am leaving."

"You cannot leave. You are in detention."

"I can will myself to leave," he said. "You cannot hold me in place."

"Our machinery will hold—"

"Your machinery is dreams," Reuter said, "dreams which you have willed and which I deny. Good-bye," he said, "good-bye." And he vaulted himself out of there at enormous speed and height. The Directors dwindled, and the cubicle in which they had held him became little more than a mote in the dreaming, tormented eye of the universe.

Very little to do now. Very little more, and then he could bequeath at last past to the present, joined forever in all of the darkness and force that the machines had, at last, unsuccessfully denied. No more of this, no more. He went to Vienna and—

Prestissimo

As the last notes of the movement, the ascending scale, split the hall, he rose, rose from his position between the contrabassi, waved his arms, addressed them. "You can do anything you want to do," he said. "It is all within your hands."

They murmured in disbelief.

"No," he said. "No, it's true!"

They looked at him with the aspect of animals whose cages for the first time were suddenly being tugged open.

"Liberation!" Reuter shouted. "Freedom, the freedom of our history! Don't you understand that all of the time it was just us; it was just all of us on this plain, all of humanity? Do it!" he shouted. "Do it, do it!"

And the audience were on their feet, first a few, then by the hundreds, the last stragglers coming up then, the orchestra too, the chorus beginning to jump up and down on the racks, racks heaving, the hall shaking, the conductor crying vainly for control. Shouts began.

"It's true!" Reuter said. "It's true. You dreamed the past, you can undream the present; in our humanity we can contain everything! Everything!" he said, and the shouts overwhelmed him. There was no way that he could be heard now, not that he needed to be heard. It was done, it was done. It was finished. He sped from the hall singing, leaving behind him all of the mad and wondrous pieces of the past ready, finally, to be made sacrament.

No question about it, once you saw the truth, matters were never quite the same again.

No question about it.

He could do anything now that he wanted to do.

And he did.

Epilogue

Enough of this self-pitying nonsense, Reuter said, and threw the Heiligenstadt Testament into the fire and went out of his rooms and dwelt in love and feeling for the rest of his days, writing many masterworks, not the least of which was the immortal and still-remembered Tenth Symphony.